Antonio S
and the
MYSTERY
of THEODORE
GUZMAN

First published 1997 by
Allen & Unwin Pty Ltd
9 Atchison Street
St Leonards NSW 1590
Australia
Phone: (61 2) 8425 0100
Fax: (61 2) 9906 2218
E-mail: frontdesk@allen-unwin.com.au
Web: http://www.allen-unwin.com.au

National Library of Australia
Cataloguing-in Publication entry:
Hirsch, Odo.
Antonio S and the mystery of Theodore Guzman.
ISBN 1 86448 409 8.
I. Title.
A823.3

Cover and text designed and typeset by Ruth Grüner
Cover illustration by Andrew McLean
Printed in Australia by Australian Print Group

7 9 10 8 6

ODO HIRSCH'S books for children include *Antonio S and the Mystery of Theodore Guzman*, *Bartlett and the Ice Voyage* and *Hazel Green*.

His first book, *Antonio S and the Mystery of Theodore Guzman*, was immediately popular with children and adults. It was short-listed for the 1998 National Children's Literature Award at the Festival Awards for Literature, was an Honour Book in the 1998 Children's Book Council Book of the Year – Younger Readers Awards, and won the inaugural Patricia Wrightson Prize for Children's Literature in the 1999 NSW Premier's Literary Awards.

Odo Hirsch was born in Australia where he studied medicine and worked as a doctor. He now lives in London. His books have been translated into several languages.

'*Strange, delicate and delightful*' Philip Pullman, GUARDIAN

'*A highly unusual little book written with elegant economy . . . More down to earth than St Exupery's* The Little Prince *but has something of its clear-eyed wisdom. Don't miss it.*' Christina Hardyment, INDEPENDENT

'*In this magical story, wonderfully developed characters, many literary references and a lyrical prose combine to provide a captivating insight into the creative imagination.*' READING TIME

'*Something out of the ordinary*' Robin Morrow, WEEKEND AUSTRALIAN

'*A truly brilliant account of how a play is made*' THE TIMES

Antonio S

and the MYSTERY
of THEODORE GUZMAN

Odo Hirsch

Illustrations by
ANDREW McLEAN

ALLEN & UNWIN

Antonio S was a boy who knew all sorts of things. His father was a magician and his mother was a doctor. So even though Antonio was only ten, he already knew things that some people never learn in a whole lifetime. He could hop backwards in a perfectly straight line with his eyes closed and his arms folded in front of him, and he could tell whether a person had measles just by looking inside his or her mouth. He could juggle three oranges and make a fourth one appear out of his sleeve. He knew how to listen to the sounds of a person's heartbeat. And these were only some of the things Antonio knew.

Antonio's father was called Scarrabo the Magnificent and his mother was Professor Kettering. There was hardly a day when Professor Kettering was not called urgently to see someone who was sick in the city. Scarrabo the Magnificent was not only a magician, he was an escape artist as well.

Scarrabo's most famous escape was called the Pendulum Escape. First his wrists were handcuffed and his legs were strapped, his elbows and knees were pulled together and locked by three separate chains, and then, bundled up as tight as a radish, he was put into a potato sack and hung upside down in the air. Then the potato sack was given a mighty push and it swung back and forth, just like the pendulum on a gigantic grandfather clock. That was how Scarrabo had to get out of it.

It was no problem for the great escape artist to free himself from the chains and locks, even when he was hanging upside down, but all the swinging made it a terribly difficult feat. It took so much out of him that he performed it only once every four months, and he could barely manage to get out of bed the next day.

When people heard that Scarrabo the Magnificent was going to perform the Pendulum Escape, they came from all over to watch. The best spot for the escape was a bridge high above a river. The sack swung to and fro in the wind, and when Scarrabo released himself he dropped with a perfect double somersault, diving into the water with barely a splash. His assistants, Walter Flood and Louisa Roberts, would be waiting in a boat to fish him out, because by the time Scarrabo had performed the escape and finished his dive he was too exhausted to swim.

Antonio himself did not see the Pendulum Escape until he was six. But he would never forget that day. The sack was swinging so long he began to wonder whether Scarrabo was ever going to get out of it. Professor Kettering, who was standing with him on the riverbank, didn't seem nervous at all.

'I'd say by now he's working on the second last chain,' she said calmly, as they watched the sack still swinging high in the wind.

'What happens if he can't get out?' asked Antonio.

Professor Kettering laughed. 'Last chain now,' she said a moment later, 'and . . . he's finished.'

But there was no sign of Scarrabo.

'Why doesn't he come out?' demanded Antonio.

'Wait,' said Professor Kettering.

All along the riverbank, on the bridge, sitting in boats, people were watching the sack flying back and forth in the air. There was not a sound to be heard, as if everyone in the crowd were hypnotised by the swinging object.

Professor Kettering whispered to Antonio: 'He'll wait a minute longer. No one can judge suspense like Scarrabo.'

And sure enough, one minute later, just when some people were beginning to think that Scarrabo had failed and others were imagining that he had not been put into the sack at all, an arm appeared through the top of the sack, and then another arm, and an instant later the sack collapsed and there was the figure of Scarrabo in midair, falling, diving, turning a perfect double somersault and disappearing into the water with barely a splash.

Antonio lived in a great house that had belonged to a duke in the days when there were still kings and queens and dukes and duchesses. In those days, rich people travelled in carriages and poor people walked, and the house had been deep in the country, a full day's ride away from the town. A famous designer had been called in to plan the gardens and parks around the house, which stretched far in every direction.

That was a long time ago. There were no longer dukes and duchesses. Now the old duke's country house was less than an hour's ride by car from the middle of the town. And the town itself had got bigger, turning into a city. More and more people lived there and more and more houses were built. Slowly the city crept outwards, swallowing the empty land until it came right up to the walls of the house, just as the incoming tide eventually reaches a sandcastle that has been built all alone on a beach.

But what a house it was to live in! How could such a place, where many families now lived, have been built for just *one* duke? It had the shape of an enormous square that was as big as a football field in each direction, and it was three storeys high. In the middle was a gigantic courtyard and the entrance was a tall archway. A broad, sweeping stairway rose to the upper floors.

There were four fountains in the courtyard. Each fountain was in the shape of a different animal, and the most beautiful was a dolphin that blew water from its mouth in a graceful arc over its own tail. The stone of the fountains was worn smooth by the water that had been sprayed over them for years and years.

The great house had one square tower. It rose at the corner where Antonio's family lived. The entrance to the tower was from a staircase right outside Antonio's bedroom.

There were two rooms and a loft in the tower, one on top of the other. Each of the rooms had a window in each of its walls, so you could look at the view in every direction—at the city on one side, and at the country on the other. The first room in the tower was Professor Kettering's study and it was lined with bookcases from floor to ceiling. Here, at a large desk made out of rich brown wood, Professor Kettering wrote her medical books. A skeleton stood in one corner of the room. This was the skeleton that Professor Kettering had used when she was a student at the university. Antonio often spent time examining it while his mother worked at the desk, and he could name twenty-seven of the thirty-two bones that make up the human arm.

The top room of the tower was Scarrabo's invention room. Here his greatest tricks were thought up. Scarrabo's invention room was like one big box bulging with fascinating and unexpected discoveries. Sometimes there was barely space to walk from one side to the other. There were cupboards full of costumes and chests full of magical instruments, cages full of the rabbits Scarrabo pulled out of his hat and the pigeons he produced from the folds of his cape. Handcuffs and chains were draped across the floor and hung on the walls. The swords that Louisa Roberts pushed into the box in Scarrabo's sword-skewering trick stood in the corners. There were cards on the tables and stacks of plates to juggle and there were piles of magic books on the floor and shelfloads of books over the windows. And in the loft above the invention room there were more cupboards and chests with special equipment which Scarrabo brought down only for the most complicated tricks.

Sometimes, after he had spent an hour looking through Professor Kettering's medical books, Antonio climbed the stairs to Scarrabo's invention room. You might have thought that the best time to go there would have been when no one else was around, and Antonio could have had all the instruments and costumes to himself. But it wasn't. The best time was when Scarrabo and Louisa Roberts and Walter Flood were all there.

Walter and Louisa were themselves gifted magicians, although they were not accomplished performers like Scarrabo. They preferred to invent and perfect tricks rather than to be the centre of attention. And when they invented, the instruments in the room came alive and did things that Antonio would never have even imagined.

When Antonio went up to Scarrabo's invention room he sat on a chest against a wall as the three magicians experimented and planned. The process of thinking up a new trick was not clear to Antonio, and Scarrabo himself could not explain it very well. Everyone had his own way of inventing, and it took great concentration.

Walter Flood would walk around and around the room with a frown on his face, bumping into boxes and dragging chains that got caught on his feet, fiddling with a spongy leather ball which was always appearing from his shirt cuffs, from his trouser legs, from his collar, from behind his ear, from beneath the sole of his foot. Sometimes he would make it appear from under Antonio's armpit without stopping for even a second as he passed by on his way around the room.

Louisa Roberts concentrated by sitting at a small table beside one of the windows and practising intricate tricks with matchsticks and thimbles.

And Scarrabo juggled. Five, six, seven plates, the more plates he juggled the harder he was thinking. If a particularly wonderful idea struck him while he was juggling, the plates hit the floor with a crash. No one objected. The day Scarrabo invented the Shadow Disappearance Trick the floor was covered with broken china, and at dinner he happily announced to Professor Kettering that he had broken nine plates.

Nine plates was the record. Scarrabo had never broken as many again. But if you saw the Shadow Disappearance Trick, you would understand why.

The tower was the best part of the old house that had belonged to the duke. It was the strongest part, the Last

Resort. Scarrabo the Magnificent knew all kinds of stories about it. During one of the wars, Scarrabo said, when an enemy earl had attacked the house, the duke and his men were forced to retreat there. Below them, the entire house was in the hands of their opponents. But the earl couldn't get into the tower. The duke and his men defended the staircase. There were still scratches on the banister where one man after another had tried to climb the staircase and had been cut down. Eventually the duke and his men had fought their way back out of the tower and recaptured the house room by room, driving the earl out.

Scarrabo told this story one night when they were having dinner.

'So the earl and his men were down here?' asked Antonio.

'Yes,' said Scarrabo, 'they ate in this very room, and the earl slept in your bedroom.'

'Nonsense, Scarrabo,' said Professor Kettering, who rarely believed the stories Scarrabo told. 'Those scratches on the banister come from taking furniture up and down those horrible stairs. You and Walter should take more care with those chests you're always moving around.'

Scarrabo the Magnificent didn't say anything to that. But later he showed Antonio the deep cut that the duke himself had made with his sword as he fled backwards up the stairs into the tower, defending himself as he went.

Scarrabo knew other things about the house. There were secret passages, and tunnels, and doors that looked like doors but were really walls, and walls that looked like walls but were really doors. Professor Kettering didn't believe that either.

'Where are these secret passages and tunnels, Scarrabo?' she would ask.

Scarrabo didn't know. No one knew. The plans for such a house are destroyed after it is finished, and only one or two people ever know all its secrets.

Antonio thought that the duke's house was the perfect house for an escape artist to live in, full of secret entrances and exits, just like a trick. And if its mysteries made it the perfect house for an escape artist to live in, they made it the perfect house for the son of that escape artist to explore.

CHAPTER 2

Lots of families lived in Duke's House. Its long corridors and endless rows of rooms had been divided into separate apartments, some large, some small, each one different from the others. Antonio knew most of the people, but there were some who kept themselves to themselves and didn't even come out for a walk in summer. If there was one person who knew *everyone* who lived in Duke's House it was Mr Carman, the caretaker. Mr Carman's apartment was on the ground floor right next to the entrance to the courtyard.

There were always jobs for Mr Carman to do around the great house. For instance, every spring he turned off the water in the fountains for a day and scraped away the moss that had grown there over the previous year. All the children in the house watched as he did it. After he turned off the water Mr Carman would wait for five minutes before draining the fountains, and everyone was allowed to bring a glass jar or a bucket and save the tadpoles that lived in the fountains. You weren't supposed to tip the tadpoles back into the fountains after Mr Carman turned the water on again, but everyone did.

On the second floor of Duke's House lived Ralph Robinson and his family. Ralph Robinson was the oldest and he had three brothers and a baby sister and all of them had names that began with R. In addition to Ralph there was Richard, Ronald, Randolph and the baby girl was called Rhonda. This made it easy for Ralph's mother, because she didn't have to sew on new initials when the children grew out of their clothes and handed them down to the others.

Ralph Robinson was in Antonio's class at school and he was Antonio's best friend. Every day they walked out through the archway of Duke's House together, across the lawn, down the street and around the corner, through the park, and down another couple of streets to the school gate. Ralph's brothers Richard and Ronald came with them.

The most important thing about Ralph Robinson was the amount he could eat. Every day he brought four sandwiches, two apples, and three pieces of cake to school in his lunch box, and even after all that he was still able to mop up everyone else's leftovers. All the other Robinson children ate half as much and were twice as fat. Ralph was as thin as a stick. No one could match Ralph Robinson when it came to eating. Everyone thought he was amazing, and Ralph himself was very proud of his ability. But he was reluctant to go far from home without a full lunch box in his hand. The one thing that really worried Ralph Robinson was not know-ing where his next meal was coming from.

Sometimes Antonio played with Ralph Robinson after school. When it was warm they went out onto the lawn in front of the house, or into the small wood that was just behind it, where they played a game of surpris-ing each other in ambushes. The first one to spot the other tried to jump on him without warning and wrestle him to the ground. Ralph was so thin he could hide himself completely behind a tree trunk and you didn't know you had found him until he gave a blood-curdling yell and jumped on top of you. Antonio was not as thin as Ralph, so he had to crouch down and hide behind bushes. Crouching behind a bush was never as good as stand-ing up straight behind a tree trunk. By the time you leapt up to jump on somebody they almost always saw you coming.

Ralph Robinson didn't necessarily believe the stories about secret passages and tunnels that Scarrabo told. He was more inclined to be on Professor Kettering's side.

'Anyway,' said Ralph, '*my* father says that by the time they built the house, dukes had stopped fighting wars. So they wouldn't need tunnels.'

'Dukes *never* stopped fighting wars,' said Antonio.

'Of course they did,' said Ralph, 'otherwise they'd still be fighting them today.'

They were sitting on a log in the wood. Ralph had just jumped on Antonio for the fifth time that afternoon and Antonio was getting sick of the game. He picked up a couple of tiny pine cones and began practising a trick he had seen Walter Flood perform in Scarrabo's invention room. You rested the cone on your left palm, put your right thumb and index finger on it and gave it a spin, then with a flourish turned your right hand over to show *two* cones sitting on it. The key to the trick was to have the second cone ready underneath your left hand, held ever so gently by its tip between your thumb and index finger, so that it was just out of sight.

Walter Flood didn't use tiny pine cones when he performed the trick in the invention room. He used gooseberries, and every time the two gooseberries appeared in his right hand he popped them both in his mouth. It was a simple trick, much too simple for an experienced magician like Walter Flood, and the only reason he did it was as a way of eating gooseberries. If there was a way of getting magic into anything, you could be sure that Walter Flood would do it.

'It's no good. I can see what you're doing,' said Ralph.

Anyone could have seen what Antonio was doing. He hadn't got it right yet.

20

'Doesn't matter if dukes *didn't* fight wars any more,' said Antonio. 'They'd still want to be prepared. They'd still need a few tricks up their sleeves.'

'Maybe,' said Ralph, keeping his eyes on Antonio's hands.

Finally Antonio did the trick. The cone disappeared from his left hand, and two appeared in his right.

'Very good,' said Ralph. Ralph never tried tricks, even though he had seen Antonio practise five or six and knew exactly how they worked.

'You must be hungry,' said Antonio.

'Yes,' said Ralph.

'Did you know that people eat the seeds in pine cones?'

'Really?'

'Oh yes,' said Antonio. 'There are explorers in the forest who lived on them after their food ran out. You can live on pine nuts for days and days.'

Ralph picked up one of the pine cones and tried to pull the segments apart. The cones were very small and green. It took him five minutes to get a single seed out. Ralph looked doubtfully at the tiny yellow particle on the end of his finger. Antonio watched him put it in his mouth. Ralph's face screwed up.

'Of course, they don't taste as bitter if you roast them first,' said Antonio, jumping to his feet.

Ralph chased him all the way home, crashing through

the trees behind him. But even though Ralph Robinson was tall and thin, he wasn't a fast runner. Antonio beat him home easily.

Antonio still wondered about the secret passages and false doors in the great house that the duke had built. What did Ralph Robinson's father know compared to Scarrabo the Magnificent? He probably wouldn't even recognise a secret passage if he fell into one. It took someone who really knew about escapes, about disappearances and miraculous comebacks, to understand a house like that.

And eventually Antonio did discover something. It was not exactly a secret passage or a trick fireplace, but it was a small door and it looked as if it had been made so that no one would notice it. And a door that is made so that no one will notice it must lead somewhere unusual. Antonio didn't need Scarrabo to tell him that!

CHAPTER 3

The door that Antonio found was a few steps from Mr Carman's apartment. It was a small, narrow opening beneath the staircase that led to the upper floors, not much taller than Antonio himself, and it just happened to be standing slightly ajar one day. Antonio had passed that spot hundreds, maybe thousands of times before. At first he wondered whether it was a new door that Mr Carman had just cut in the wall. But the next morning, when he went out through the archway again on his way to school and glanced at the spot, there was no sign of it. The door had vanished. The wall under the stairs looked just as it always did: big blocks of roughened stone with deep grooves between them.

That day, Antonio couldn't wait for his last lesson to end. After school he ran almost all the way home without even waiting for Ralph Robinson. And sure enough, when you went right up to the wall, you could see that there *was* a door. There was a narrow crack, no wider than a toothpick, that ran up and across and down the other side over the grooves in the stone. How carefully it had been made! If you were more than a few steps away you couldn't see it at all. And if someone had not forgotten to shut it for a few minutes Antonio would never even have known that it was there. But how did you open it?

Antonio put his fingers into one of the grooves and pulled. The door did not budge even a millimetre. Antonio looked closer. His nose almost touched the stone. He got down on his knees, still looking. He could find no handle, no lever. But then he noticed a tiny lock, no bigger than a thumbnail, underneath the ridge of one of the blocks of stone. You would never spot it unless you were down on your knees, peering at the wall, like Antonio.

The lock looked very old. The metal had turned green. But it must still work, the door had been open only yesterday. If only he had the key. There must be a key.

Antonio heard footsteps behind him. He jumped up. Mr Carman, who was dragging one of his rakes across the courtyard, had spotted him. Antonio ran out through the archway and all the way around the house until he came to the wood.

He sat on a log and thought. If anyone had the key to the door it would be Mr Carman.

Scarrabo the Magnificent was not at all surprised to hear about the door. It was almost as if he had expected just such a thing.

'That's a very common place for a secret passage to come out,' he explained. 'Just imagine, Antonio, if your enemies have arrived to seize you. What do you do? You make them follow you into the house and then, once they have rushed up the stairs—*Pfffff!*—you disappear through a fireplace and come out from the secret passage at the bottom of the staircase. They'll spend the next two days looking for you in every cupboard, but you'll be long gone. If your timing is right, you escape from under their very noses.'

Scarrabo the Magnificent knew all about timing. Every trick, every escape depended on it.

'It's probably the door to Mr Carman's broom cupboard,' said Professor Kettering.

That was another possibility.

Antonio S wanted to know what was behind the door. Eventually he thought of a plan. But in order for the plan to work he needed another person. So he told Ralph Robinson about the door.

Ralph Robinson said: 'Why don't we just ask Mr Carman what's behind the door? He knows everything about this house.'

Ralph was right. Mr Carman knew all there was to know about the old house. He couldn't have done his job properly otherwise. But the idea of just asking Mr Carman didn't appeal to Antonio. He didn't just want to *ask* what was behind the door. He wanted to *see*.

'Mr Carman wouldn't tell us, if it was a secret passage,' said Antonio. 'He wouldn't want us to know.'

'And what if it *is* just his broom cupboard?' asked Ralph Robinson.

'He still wouldn't tell. People might steal his brooms.'

Ralph looked at Antonio doubtfully.

'No, there's only one way to find out,' said Antonio. 'It's all right, Ralph. All *you* have to do is eat biscuits.'

'Oh, I'm good at that,' said Ralph cheerfully.

'I know,' said Antonio.

This was Antonio's plan. The next time Antonio saw that the stone door had been left open, Ralph Robinson was supposed to find Mr Carman and ask for biscuits.

Everyone in Duke's House was used to the sight of Ralph Robinson asking for biscuits. Sometimes Ralph ate so much at home that there was barely enough left for his baby sister, and Mrs Robinson locked him out and wouldn't give him anything else until dinner. That could be a long time to wait, too long for Ralph. The only time Professor Kettering had made the mistake of letting him into her kitchen he ate for a whole hour without stopping. He didn't talk, he didn't get up to look around, he didn't pause for breath. Almost everyone in Duke's House gave Ralph Robinson biscuits, but no one would let him into their kitchen.

So, according to Antonio's plan, when Ralph asked

for biscuits, Mr Carman would go into his kitchen, asking Ralph to wait for him. And that would give Antonio just enough time to slip behind the secret door, explore for a couple of minutes, and slip out again before Mr Carman came back to lock it.

Antonio glanced at the door every time he used the staircase. He came down and checked whenever he could. A whole month passed and he had almost given up hope when he saw the gap in the wall once more. The door was standing ajar. He turned in an instant, raced back up the stairs, met Ralph Robinson on the second flight and dragged him down. They stopped at the bottom, just out of sight of Mr Carman's apartment.

'Just ask for biscuits,' Antonio whispered.

'How many?'

'As many as you can get.'

'I always take as many as I can get.'

'Just eat until I come back, then,' whispered Antonio impatiently.

'How long will that be?'

'How should I know? What difference does it make?'

'I need to know how quickly to eat the biscuits.'

Antonio gave Ralph a push. 'Go on. He'll come out and lock the door before we even have a chance, if you keep talking.'

Ralph went and knocked on Mr Carman's front door.

Antonio crouched at the bottom of the stairs, listening. He heard the door open.

'Hello, Mr Carman,' said Ralph. 'I was wondering if you have any biscuits you don't need.'

Antonio heard Mr Carman's familiar voice. 'Do you want to feed them to the birds, Ralph?'

'Not exactly.'

Mr Carman laughed. 'Mrs Carman has gone out. I don't know if we have any left.'

'Please, Mr Carman,' said Ralph in his hungriest voice.

'All right, Ralph,' said Mr Carman. 'Stay here, and I'll see what I can find.'

Antonio waited a few seconds longer. Then he jumped to his feet and ran as fast as he could around the bottom of the staircase. He could see Ralph standing in front of Mr Carman's apartment. But Ralph didn't even notice as Antonio cautiously opened the stone door and disappeared behind it. Ralph was hoping that Mr Carman would come back soon. All this talk of biscuits had made him hungry.

CHAPTER 4

Antonio was in a small room with a bare stone floor.

Professor Kettering was wrong, it wasn't the room where Mr Carman kept his brooms. It was where he kept some old tins of paint, a couple of boxes of tools, a few scraps of wood, a bench that he used for sawing planks, and other things as well. But no brooms.

The bench was right in front of the door, and Antonio almost fell over it as he came in.

There was a bare light bulb hanging from the ceiling.

Antonio switched it on and shut the door behind him. In fact, the door was not made of stone at all, but of wood that had been cleverly designed to look like stone from the outside. On the other side of the room, an old wheelbarrow stood upright against the wall, balancing on its wheel. The paint had flaked off its handles and there were rusty holes in its tray. Beside it, there was a narrow opening, not much more than a slit in the wall through which a person could pass if he turned himself sideways.

People must have been thin in the old duke's days, Antonio thought when he spotted the opening, if their secret passages had entrances that were that small.

He didn't have much time. Not even Ralph Robinson could keep Mr Carman occupied forever. He stepped around the bench and over a tool box, past the wheel-barrow, and went into the opening at the back of the room.

He was at the start of a dark, narrow corridor. As he walked, the light coming from the room behind him grew dim. It was like being in the wood at twilight, when he and Ralph Robinson stayed out too late. His eyes became accustomed to the darkness. The corridor was rough. The stone slabs on the floor were any old size and they weren't perfectly flat, the bricks in the walls had been slapped together without worrying too much if one came out further than another. The walls curved over and made a ceiling not far above his head. Pieces of plaster and fragments of brick were scattered on the floor.

If this was a secret passage, thought Antonio, the people who built it should have cleaned up the floor. You could easily trip over those pieces if you were trying to escape in a hurry.

Antonio continued along the corridor. He tried to work out what direction it was taking. It must be running towards the side of the house. He had not imagined that a secret passage would look like this. He expected secret doors, or escape hatches in the floor, or a staircase leading down from a room. But there was nothing like that. In fact, the corridor came to a dead end not much further along. In the darkness, Antonio could make out a brick wall with a pile of rubble in front of it, and that was all.

He stopped.

Something else had caught his attention. There was a very thin band of light on the wall beside him. Antonio put up his hand. The light fell across his fingers. He looked to see where it was coming from. There was a crack between the bricks in the other wall.

The crack couldn't have been much bigger than a pencil. Antonio put his eye right up to the bricks and peered through it.

ODORE

GUZMAN

tars in

AMLET

at the

LO THEATRE

That was all he could see. Antonio frowned. He tried looking with the other eye, but he couldn't see any more.

The words were in big gold letters. They stood out against a bright red background.

Antonio stared at them. Odore Guzman? What was an Odore Guzman?

There was a Mr Guzman who lived on the ground floor of the house. He hardly ever came out of his apartment, and when he did come out he never went further than the main entrance. He walked with the creaky walk of an old man, and he always wore a blue Homburg hat, whatever the weather. All the children in Duke's House thought this was a very funny name for a hat, and that anyone who wore it should have an equally funny title. 'The Homburger was out today,' they would tell each other, if someone had seen Mr Guzman on one of his creaky strolls to the main

32

entrance. But the Homburger was one of those people whom you laugh about from a distance. No one would ever have dared go near him if they saw him walking across the courtyard.

Time was passing but Antonio continued to peer through the crack. He couldn't drag himself away. There was something fascinating and inviting, something spectacular about those gold words and their bold red background, as if an amazing story stood behind them. Antonio stared and stared. The words made him think of light and noise, music, laughter and applause. And yet here, in the secret passage where he stood, everything was so dark and quiet.

Suddenly, something black passed across the words. For a second it blocked them out, and then it was gone.

Antonio jumped back. Suddenly he understood everything. He had been looking into a room in the Homburger's apartment. The letters must be part of a poster that was hanging on the wall. And the person who had crossed in front of the poster must be the Homburger himself!

Antonio's heart was pounding. What would the Homburger do if he had seen him? But he couldn't have seen him, not in that instant. And he hadn't even stopped to look through the crack. But what if he had come back and were looking *now*? Antonio scrambled away towards the entrance of the passage. But something was different. He stopped. Where was the entrance? Everything was dark, completely dark. There was no light coming from the wheelbarrow room. Someone must have come in and turned it off.

So much for Ralph Robinson's help!

Antonio looked back at the crack in the Homburger's wall for a moment. The thin yellow beam coming out of it was the only light left in the passage now. He turned and began to move gingerly along the corridor. Fragments of brick and plaster slipped under his feet. He stayed close to the wall, feeling his way with his hand.

Eventually he made it back to the wheelbarrow room. The feel of the wall changed from rough brick to smooth plaster. He paused, trying to remember where things were in the room. He began to move forward very, very cautiously, feeling his way. Then he could see a band of light, like the thinnest ribbon of silver, under the door on the other side. He heaved a sigh of relief. With his next step he put his foot straight through a pile of empty paint cans.

The cans collapsed with a clang. It sounded like the loudest noise the world had ever heard. He froze. One of the cans rolled across the floor for a long time before it finally came to rest with a dull thud.

Antonio inched forward, sliding each foot carefully over the ground to avoid kicking anything else over. He felt a toolbox with his toe and stepped over that. He remembered the bench for sawing planks and felt his way around it. At last he reached the door and pushed against it.

The door didn't open. Antonio pushed harder. Still it stayed firmly shut. It was locked.

Antonio leaned against it. How was he going to get out? Who knew how often Mr Carman came in here to get one of his tools? Maybe not for weeks at a time. As for Ralph Robinson, give him a scrap to put in his mouth and he forgot about everything else in the world. He could be here for weeks!

What would Scarrabo the Magnificent do in this situation? He would pick the lock on the door. Give Scarrabo a hairpin or even a toothpick and he would pick any lock. He would be out of here in thirty seconds. That was what Scarrabo the Magnificent would do.

But that wasn't much help to Antonio. Lock-picking was something Scarrabo had not taught him yet.

Antonio remembered the light bulb and switched it on. As if that were the signal that someone had been waiting for, there was a click behind him and the door opened.

Antonio turned around, still blinking and shielding his eyes after the darkness. Mr Carman was standing in the doorway, his arms folded across his chest.

'So, Antonio,' he said, '*this* is what Ralph Robinson and his biscuits were about.'

Antonio didn't say anything.

'Come out,' said Mr Carman.

Antonio came out. Mr Carman closed the door.

'Don't you have to lock it?' demanded Antonio.

'It locks itself as soon as you close it. In fact, Antonio, you locked yourself in.' Mr Carman grinned. 'No one has tried to play a trick like that on me for years. I should have known it would be you, Antonio. Who shall I tell? Your mother? Your father? Walter Flood, perhaps?'

'Tell whoever you like,' said Antonio miserably. 'I don't care.'

'Oh ho!' said Mr Carman, laughing. 'What did you find there?'

'Nothing.'

'Nothing. I could have told you there would be nothing. But you wanted to find out for yourself, didn't you?'

Antonio didn't say anything.

'And without even taking a torch? You didn't think of that, eh? Do you imagine that secret passages have lights everywhere, just for convenience?'

'Is it a secret passage, Mr Carman?' said Antonio with excitement, forgetting that Mr Carman had just discovered him hiding there. 'Is that what it is?'

Mr Carman began to walk towards one of the fountains in the courtyard where the water was not running properly.

'I don't know,' he said, 'it doesn't go anywhere.'

'No, but maybe it did once,' said Antonio, running beside him.

'Maybe,' said Mr Carman.

'Don't you know?'

'This house has been changed so many times, Antonio, no one knows every detail of what was here originally. Next time, ask me, yes? Maybe we can investigate together.'

Mr Carman began to inspect the fountain. It was in the shape of a horse splashing through waves and tossing his head back. The water was supposed to surge out of the horse's mouth, but there was only a trickle. Mr Carman turned off the water at a tap under a hatch in the ground and began to unscrew the pipe in the horse's mouth. Antonio watched.

'Off you go, Antonio,' Mr Carman said over his shoulder. 'If you stay here much longer, I'll make you do some work!'

Antonio found Ralph Robinson, who had given up trying to find *him* and was just about to go to the park to look for frogs near the duckpond.

'You should be ashamed of yourself,' Antonio told him. 'You didn't keep Mr Carman occupied for more than five minutes.'

Ralph didn't feel the slightest bit guilty. 'Mr Carman's biscuits weren't very nice. In fact, Mrs Carman had just gone to buy some fresh ones.'

'So?'

'So it was hard to pretend I was enjoying them. I ate six or seven, but I couldn't go on. They'd all gone soft. What happened to you, anyway?'

'I got locked in,' said Antonio. He didn't tell Ralph exactly *who* had locked him in.

Ralph grinned. 'Did Mr Carman find you?'

'Of course he found me. How do you think I got out?'

'Oh, I don't know,' said Ralph. 'I thought maybe you did an escape.'

Ralph didn't think that at all. Ralph Robinson knew perfectly well that Scarrabo would not teach anyone an escape until they were completely grown up. Escapes were too dangerous.

'Well, I suppose you don't want to hear what I found,' said Antonio.

'What?'

'Oh, nothing.'

'What, Antonio? What?'

'Oh, nothing.'

But Ralph wouldn't believe that, and he kept asking

'What? What?' all the way to the park, and even while they were looking for frogs, and even for part of the way home again. And in a way it *was* nothing that Antonio had found, unless you count that crack in the Homburger's wall and the strange, enticing words on the poster that he had glimpsed.

CHAPTER 5

When Scarrabo the Magnificent wasn't performing, or inventing new tricks, or recovering from some exhausting performance like the Pendulum Escape, he was practising. Practise, practise, practise. That's what Scarrabo said and that's what Scarrabo did. You couldn't just turn up on the day, do a few tricks and spend the rest of your time lying in bed reading the newspaper. If you didn't practise you would get things wrong. Walter Flood and Louisa Roberts sat on a chest in the invention room and watched him more closely than any audience at his performances, and Scarrabo didn't stop practising until they were satisfied. If you could satisfy Walter Flood and Louisa Roberts, you could satisfy anyone.

Sometimes, when the weather was warm and Scarrabo felt like getting out of the invention room, he went outside to practise on the grass in front of Duke's House. The people who lived in the house got used to the sight of Scarrabo twirling his arms on the lawn and making half a dozen pigeons disappear and reappear and disappear and reappear again and again in and out of a small leather travelling bag. They got used to seeing cards and coins and coloured handkerchiefs and sharp knives and glass boxes doing impossible things in the morning sunlight. Or Scarrabo might be walking round and round the lawn, juggling a set of knives while balancing a stack of teapots on the end of his nose, followed by a procession of children who picked up anything they could find to toss from hand to hand.

There were times when Scarrabo found himself surrounded by half the children who lived in the house, and by a few of their parents as well, and what started out as practice turned into a performance all of its own. But Scarrabo the Magnificent didn't mind that. In

his opinion, it wasn't enough to practise the tricks themselves, you had to practise performing them to an audience as well.

One afternoon, a week or two after he had slipped into the secret passage and looked through the crack into the Homburger's room, Antonio went out to join his father, who was on the lawn in front of the house. There were at least ten pairs of handcuffs around him, and he was locking one pair after the other onto his wrists and getting out of them. Scarrabo was able to twist his hands out of some, and for the others he needed only the slightest implement, only the dried stem of a stalk of grass, to open the lock.

He was alone. Most people weren't interested in seeing the magician get out of ten pairs of handcuffs in a row.

Scarrabo glanced at Antonio as he sat down beside him. His hands continued to work at the pair of handcuffs he was loosening. The cuffs slipped off. Scarrabo picked up another pair, locked them on, put his hands together and did something to the locking mechanisms that Antonio could not see, and then pulled his hands apart dramatically, just as he would do in front of an audience. The handcuffs fell on the grass in front of him.

Antonio watched silently.

'What is it, Antonio?' said Scarrabo.

Antonio picked up one of the handcuffs. It was a large pair made out of black metal, and it had a warm, oily feel. Scarrabo's handcuffs were always well greased.

'Do you know who those handcuffs were used for?' said Scarrabo.

Scarrabo's handcuffs were not simply implements that had been bought from the local police station. Each pair had been used on a famous criminal, and there was a story for every one.

'Sticks Jackson,' said Antonio.

'Right,' said Scarrabo. He held out his hands. Antonio snapped the handcuffs that had been used on Sticks Jackson over Scarrabo's wrists.

Scarrabo reached into his pocket with both hands locked together and pulled out a toothpick.

'They say Sticks Jackson always had a toothpick between his lips,' he said. 'Not very good manners, that's true. But it could have saved him. If Sticks Jackson had known *this* little trick,' Scarrabo said, opening the lock of one of the cuffs and then the other with the toothpick, 'he wouldn't have spent thirty years in prison. Right?'

'Right,' said Antonio.

Antonio liked the way his father got out of Sticks Jackson's handcuffs. Scarrabo always used a toothpick, just like Sticks Jackson could have done if he had known how to use it. In his show, the audience saw him put it between his lips just before Louisa Roberts snapped the cuffs on him, and then Walter Flood, dressed as a policeman, would lead him away. But in ten seconds Scarrabo was out of the cuffs and had slipped behind a screen, and when Walter Flood looked around all he could do was take off his policeman's hat and scratch his head in amazement.

Scarrabo rubbed his wrists. Too much practice with handcuffs would make anyone's wrists sore.

'Papa, who is Mr Guzman?' asked Antonio.

Scarrabo looked surprised at the question.

'Mr Guzman, Papa,' Antonio repeated. 'He lives on the ground floor.'

'Yes. I know who Mr Guzman is, Antonio.' Scarrabo stretched out on the grass and leaned back on his elbows. 'Have you met him?'

'No. He's hardly ever outside. I don't know anyone who has met him.'

'I have,' said Scarrabo.

'Really? When?'

'A long time ago, before we came to live here.' Scarrabo smiled. 'Long before you were born, Antonio.'

'Where did you meet him?' asked Antonio.

'At the Round House Theatre. It was the very first show I did by myself. Imagine that, Antonio. *That's* how long ago it was! Of course, I wasn't exactly the biggest star in the city in those days. I used to give my performance in the afternoon, but the main event in the theatre was the play that was on in the evening. *The Captain's*

Chalice it was called.' Scarrabo laughed. 'I can still remember the name. It's funny. Every day I would say to myself, Scarrabo, why not stay back one night and watch *The Captain's Chalice*? But I never did. I never got round to it. I was always rushing home to work on more tricks. Before I knew it, time flew by, the play ended and I hadn't even seen it.'

'And Mr Guzman?' asked Antonio.

'He was the captain. In the play. It was his chalice. Don't ask me what he did with it, I have no idea.'

'Then how did you meet him?'

'Simple. We passed each other on the stairs. I was leaving the theatre after my show and he was arriving for his. In those days the Round House Theatre was owned by Jonas Russell, and when he saw us together on the landing he came rushing down and introduced us at once. That's what Jonas was like, Antonio, he always wanted everyone to be friends. Mr Guzman didn't say much. He asked me a couple of questions about my show and wished me luck very charmingly, and after a minute he went on up the stairs. To tell you the truth, Antonio, I was too tongue-tied to say anything else to him. I was just a young magician and Theodore Guzman was already a great actor. They say he never said very much. He could do anything with a speech on stage, but he was always a quiet man when he was out of the spotlight.'

When Antonio asked Professor Kettering, she got a dreamy look in her eyes just as if she were a schoolgirl again.

'Theodore Guzman, Antonio? When I was a girl, Theodore Guzman was the greatest actor there was. I can still remember seeing him in *The Horse of Wilton Manor*. Auntie Josephine took me. I can still remember the scene where the young heir's sweetheart is dying— Theodore Guzman played the heir, of course. I tell you, Antonio, I cried and cried. I admit it. I would cry again, I'm sure. Auntie Josephine cried as well. I can remember it just as if it were yesterday.' Professor Kettering sighed. 'I couldn't stop thinking about it for weeks. There were girls who dreamed about Theodore Guzman. Well, we all did, now and again.'

'Why?' asked Antonio.

Professor Kettering put down her pen. She was sitting at her desk, correcting a chapter that she was writing for one of her medical books. She smiled wistfully.

'He was so handsome. So dashing. And yet, there was something quiet about him. Even when he was on the stage. Even when he was on the stage, you felt, although he was acting, something of the real Theodore Guzman was coming through.'

'Then he couldn't have been acting,' objected Antonio, 'if it was the real Mr Guzman coming through.'

Professor Kettering laughed. 'But he *was* acting, Antonio, that was the whole point. I don't think there is anyone like him on the stage today.'

Professor Kettering daydreamed a moment longer. Then she looked at the clock. 'Goodness, is that the time? I'm supposed to be at the hospital in half an hour.'

Antonio didn't know what Scarrabo the Magnificent and Professor Kettering were talking about. Dashing, handsome, a big star, a quiet actor: who was this Theodore Guzman? Surely it wasn't the old Homburger who came out once a month and walked around creakily for ten minutes as if he were waiting for the wind to blow him over? There must be some mistake. That must be another Theodore Guzman. Maybe the one who lived in Duke's House was a cousin of the great actor, or a distant relative, or just someone who happened to have the same name.

But there was only one problem with that idea: the poster that he had seen hanging in Mr Guzman's apartment. By now, Antonio had worked out what it was. It was a poster for a play, and the star in the play was Theodore Guzman. And if the Homburger was someone who just happened to share the great actor's name, what was he doing with one of the great actor's posters on his wall?

CHAPTER 6

'Have you ever spoken to the Homburger?' Antonio asked Ralph Robinson a few days later, when they were walking home through the park.

'The Homburger?' said Ralph. 'Don't be ridiculous!'

Antonio didn't reply. He kept his eyes on the gravel path, thinking.

'Why would you want to talk to the Homburger, anyway?' Ralph said after a while, wondering if Antonio were sick. 'He's probably completely deaf, he's so old.'

Antonio looked up. 'He was a dashing actor.'

'Who? The old Homburger? How do you know?'

'Everyone knows, Ralph.'

'I didn't know!'

'You don't know lots of things.'

'Like what? Name one!'

'The capital of Belgium.'

It was true, Ralph didn't know the capital of Belgium. They had just had a geography test and that was one of the questions he had got wrong.

'All right. Name another thing!'

Ralph didn't know about the secret passage that

Antonio had found at the back of Mr Carman's wheel-barrow room, and the crack in the wall, and the poster that was hanging in the Homburger's room.

'Well, if you're so interested in the Homburger, why don't you go up to him and say Hello. Maybe he'll give you one of his hats and you can be a Homburger too!' Ralph put both his hands on Antonio's head, making them into a little hat. 'You'd look very nice as a Homburger.'

Antonio elbowed him in the stomach.

'Is that any way for a Homburger to behave?' Ralph demanded, giving Antonio a shove.

Antonio shoved him back. Ralph swung his school bag and landed a strong hit on Antonio's arm. Antonio jumped on him and they both fell on the ground. They had quite a good fight before they decided to get up and go home.

But Antonio still wondered about the Homburger. He still thought about that poster with its glittering letters, and about the dashing actor that the Homburger had been. And why *shouldn't* he just go up to him and say Hello? Scarrabo the Magnificent was a great performer, and Antonio said Hello to him all the time. Why should the Homburger mind?

The problem with the Homburger was that you hardly ever saw him. Antonio saw Scarrabo every day and even had breakfast with him. But if he waited until he saw the Homburger out in the courtyard again, he might have to wait months and months.

There was only one way to solve the problem. He would have to knock on the Homburger's door.

But it was not so easy to walk up to the Homburger's door. Not that Antonio was frightened, of course. He was not frightened of doing it, but he didn't feel terribly courageous about it either. The Homburger was not exactly the sort of old man who was going to welcome you with sweets and biscuits. He was more the sort of old man whom you ran away from and watched from afar, crouching behind the banister on the staircase. And what was he going to say? 'Excuse me, Mr Homburger, but I just happened to peek through a crack in one of your rooms and I would be very interested to know why you have a poster with gold letters there and would you mind showing it to me and telling me about it and would you also mind telling me whether you were a dashing actor and would you also mind telling me exactly what people mean when they say that an actor dashes?' No, Antonio didn't think the Homburger would be very pleased to hear *that*, especially the part about peeking through a crack in his wall.

Almost every day, when he came home from school, Antonio said to himself, Antonio, *today* you are going to go to the Homburger's apartment. But almost every day, something important cropped up just when he was ready to go. Scarrabo would urgently need him to watch a trick, for instance, or Professor Kettering would desperately need his help to pack the equipment in her medical bag. Or Ralph Robinson would come looking for him. Or he would realise that he still hadn't worked out what he was going to say when the Homburger opened the door.

Finally, one Tuesday, Antonio decided that it was now or never. He was going to go down to the Homburger's apartment after school, and he wasn't going to let anything stop him. He was going to knock on the Homburger's door and when the Homburger opened it he was going to say: 'Mr Guzman, everyone says you were a dashing actor.' That was what he was going to do, that was what he was going to say, and that was that! The Homburger himself could work out what to do next.

Antonio got home. He went into the kitchen and poured some orange juice. He sat down at the table. He swung his legs under the chair as he drank. Walter Flood came in to get a handful of gooseberries and asked if Antonio wanted to help coil Scarrabo's ropes. Antonio shook his head, although coiling ropes with Walter was always an interesting activity, because there were at least fourteen tricks you could use while doing it. There was less and less orange juice in his glass. Finally, it was

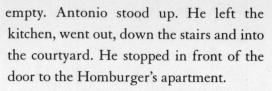

empty. Antonio stood up. He left the kitchen, went out, down the stairs and into the courtyard. He stopped in front of the door to the Homburger's apartment.

Antonio took a deep breath. The door was painted blue and there was a big gold handle at its centre. When it opened, the Homburger would be standing behind it.

He knocked.

Nothing happened.

He knocked again. He listened at the door to hear if anyone was moving inside. There was no sound.

He knocked once more, as hard as he could. The Homburger was so old, he was probably deaf.

Antonio knocked and listened, knocked and listened, for ten long minutes. He knocked as loudly as he could even though his knuckles started to get sore. But still the door did not open. Surely the Homburger wasn't out. He never went out!

Antonio was just about to start knocking for the fiftieth time when he heard a voice behind him.

'Antonio, what a noise you're making!'

Antonio turned around. It was Mr Carman.

'Mr Guzman must be deaf,' said Antonio. 'He can't hear me.'

Mr Carman laughed. 'Just because Mr Guzman is old,

it does not mean that he is deaf, Antonio. And just because he doesn't answer, it does not mean that he doesn't hear.'

'Why else wouldn't he answer?'

'Perhaps he does not wish to answer.'

'But how does he know who's there? It could be anyone.'

Mr Carman smiled. 'No, Antonio, he knows who it is. Were you watching the window? You might have caught a glimpse of him when you first knocked. He would have looked to see.'

Antonio glanced at the window near the door. It was covered in a white lace curtain.

'Come, Antonio,' said Mr Carman. 'You have knocked enough. Let's leave Mr Guzman in peace.'

Mr Carman turned to cross to the other side of the courtyard, where someone had reported that a paving stone had come loose. He took Antonio with him.

'Don't be unhappy,' Mr Carman said, resting a hand on Antonio's shoulder as they walked. 'Mr Guzman hardly sees anybody.'

'But he wouldn't mind seeing *me*, Mr Carman. I'm sure he didn't know who was there.'

Mr Carman chuckled.

Antonio looked back at the blue door. He couldn't understand why the old Homburger had refused to open it. No one had done that to him before. 'I'm just a boy!'

he said. 'Why *wouldn't* he want to see me? I'm not going to hurt him.'

'Antonio,' said Mr Carman, 'there are many people who would like to see Mr Guzman. They would like to see him just because he was a great actor, although they are not really his friends. And Mr Guzman is old now, and sometimes he is sick, and he does not wish to see people who are not his true friends. And each year the number of his true friends grows smaller, because they are old as well, and some of them have died.'

Mr Carman stopped in front of the loose paving stone. He rocked it with his foot. He knelt down and lifted one edge of the stone.

'For someone to see Mr Guzman is a great honour,' said Mr Carman, peering under the stone. 'If you are not one of his old friends, Antonio, it is almost impossible. You would have to do something special.'

'Like what?'

Mr Carman prodded the earth under the stone with a finger. 'I don't know. It would have to be so special, I cannot even imagine what you would have to do.'

Scarrabo understood Mr Guzman's problem.

'Yes, sometimes I wish I could close my door to all the people who want to talk to me,' he said. 'People always want to talk to performers. Nowadays they like to take photographs as well.'

Antonio took a cracker out of a box and fed it to one of Scarrabo's parrots.

'But you can't ignore everybody,' said Scarrabo. 'Only if you've stopped performing, like Mr Guzman. Otherwise, you can't refuse. For me, the worst time is after a show. Sometimes it takes more than an hour to get away, because of all the people who want to meet me. Maybe it was even worse for Mr Guzman. Most of us have days when the show doesn't go perfectly, but people say he never gave a bad performance. You would have to ask someone who saw him on the stage, of course.'

'Mama, did Mr Guzman ever give a bad performance?' Antonio asked Professor Kettering, when she was reading in her study.

Professor Kettering looked up from her book.

'What a strange question, Antonio,' she said. 'A bad performance? I doubt it. *I* never saw him give a bad performance. It would be much easier if you asked me if he ever gave a good performance. I saw lots of those.'

'What was his best performance?'

'His best performance?' Professor Kettering thought for a moment. 'It's always hard to say which is an actor's greatest performance, and with an actor as great as Theodore Guzman, it is even harder. Hamlet, probably.'

Antonio recognised the name at once. But his mother was not saying it properly. '*Amlet*, Mama.'

Professor Kettering laughed. '*Hamlet*, Antonio. Not

Amlet. It's a very great play about a prince whose father is killed by his uncle, who then marries his mother, but then his father's ghost comes back to tell him the truth, and there is also a girl who loves Hamlet, but Hamlet kills her father, and then she dies, and then her brother tries to kill Hamlet with the help of the uncle, but the plan doesn't work, and Hamlet kills them. And then Hamlet dies as well.'

Was she serious?

'It's a complicated play, Antonio. Would you like me to explain it again?'

'No. I don't think that will help very much.'

'Well, it's much easier to understand when you see it. Theodore Guzman played Hamlet of course. Everyone says it was his greatest performance. It was wonderful, Antonio. I was lucky that I saw it.'

'I didn't see it,' said Scarrabo, when Antonio asked him. 'I meant to, but I never got around to it. They all say it was his greatest performance. Theodore Guzman's Hamlet, they say, was the last word on the matter.'

Scarrabo was polishing one of the hollow walking sticks that he used in his shows. He waxed it until its black surface shone like oil. When he put it down, Antonio was still sitting on a chest, thinking.

'Antonio,' said Scarrabo, 'why all these questions about Mr Guzman lately? Perhaps I could ask him to meet you. He may still remember me from the time we met at the Round House Theatre. Perhaps he will agree to meet you as a favour.'

Antonio thought about this. As a favour? He shook his head.

'No?'

'No.'

Scarrabo the Magnificent clapped his hands. 'All right! Once you make a decision, stick to it! If you can't see Mr Guzman—you can't! Now, are you coming to the tailor's with me, Antonio? My new costume is ready.'

Antonio shook his head. He had not decided that he was not going to see Mr Guzman. He had decided only that he was not going to see him as a favour.

Ralph Robinson thought Antonio was acting strangely, and he told him so. For days they hadn't gone to play in the wood and Ralph hadn't had the chance to hide his stick-like body behind a tree trunk and fling it on top of Antonio. Ralph didn't think this was very fair.

'All right,' said Antonio eventually, 'let's go.'

Ralph set off eagerly around the corner of the house towards the wood. By the time Antonio arrived he had already hidden himself.

Ralph was standing behind a young oak tree. He had never hidden himself in this spot before, but he had had his eye on it for a while. The young trunk of the oak tree was just the right width to hide his skinny body. But the best thing about it was that the tree was growing on a small mound, so when Antonio passed by it would be even easier than usual for Ralph to jump on top of him and pin him to the ground. Ralph couldn't wait for Antonio to come walking through the bushes.

Ralph barely breathed. His body was as still as the trees, perhaps even stiller. He listened with all the power of his ears for the first sound of Antonio approaching.

He listened for five minutes. It seemed much longer. Nothing happened.

Finally a leaf rustled and a twig snapped.

A sly smile came over Ralph's face. Antonio was always so careless when he moved through the wood!

Ralph got ready to pounce, but he didn't get the chance. It was only Mr Carman's brown labrador. The dog stopped, gave Ralph an inquisitive look, sniffed around the ground, and disappeared again, following the scent of a squirrel.

Everything was still again. Another ten long minutes went by.

Ralph got sick of listening. Maybe this is a new trick Antonio's trying, he thought. Maybe he's planning to make me wait so long that I'll leave my hiding place, and then he'll jump on *me*. Well, we'll see about that. I can wait longer than anyone!

Ralph gave up a couple of minutes later. He couldn't bear it any more. He crept cautiously around the tree trunk, alert for the sound of Antonio S hurtling at him through the air. He crept back towards the edge of the wood.

There was Antonio. He wasn't even hiding! Ralph could easily have jumped all over him. But he didn't move. Something made him stay where he was.

Antonio was sitting on a log, staring very hard at a twig in his hand.

Ralph folded his arms across his chest. He coughed loudly. Antonio looked up with a start.

'Antonio, I don't think this is how we play the game,' Ralph said sternly. 'I don't think this game is called Sit on the Log.'

Antonio grinned.

'Ralph,' he said, 'we have to put on a play.'

'A play?'

'A play,' said Antonio.

A play? What for? What did Antonio know about putting on a play?

'Don't forget who my father is,' Antonio told Ralph. 'Scarrabo the Magnificent gives performances all the time.'

'Then put on a magic show,' answered Ralph, sitting down beside him.

'No.'

'Why?'

'Because I don't want to put on a magic show,' replied

Antonio. Mr Guzman had been a great actor. Only a play would be special enough for him. 'It has to be a play,' he repeated.

'And just where do you think you are going to perform this play?' demanded Ralph Robinson, who was beginning to wish he hadn't come out from behind the oak trunk.

'I'm not sure yet. I'll have to think about that.'

'You could put it on here in the wood. I just saw Mr Carman's dog. I'm sure she'd like to see your play.'

'Very funny,' said Antonio, getting up from the log. He set off for the house. Ralph Robinson followed him back.

CHAPTER 7

For the next couple of days Antonio didn't say anything about the play. Ralph Robinson began to think he had forgotten his crazy idea. But Antonio hadn't forgotten. In fact, he hardly thought about anything else. And the more he thought about it, the more things he had to work out. For instance, who would act with him in the play? And what play would they put on? How would they choose it? It couldn't be just any old play. It had to say the right things. If Mr Guzman was going to take notice of it, it had to have the right meanings. Was there any play that would be perfectly right?

And where, where would they stage it? It had to be at Duke's House, that was one thing Antonio knew for sure. It had to be somewhere near the house if Mr Guzman was going to see it.

Antonio put up a sign at school. It said: If you want to be in a play, speak to Antonio S.

The first person who responded was Simon Greene. Antonio should have know that would happen. Simon Greene was two years older than him and already he thought that he was an important actor. He got that idea from his parents. Simon Greene was always first to be chosen for the school pantomimes. Everyone said it wouldn't be long before his parents sent him to a drama school.

Simon Greene came up and said: 'What's this play you're advertising?' He spoke as if Antonio would be lucky to have him in the play.

Antonio said: 'I don't know yet.'

Simon Greene laughed. 'Where are you putting it on?'

'I'm not sure,' Antonio replied.

Simon Greene laughed some more. He was still laughing when he walked away. By the end of the day the whole school knew that Antonio S had advertised a play that didn't exist. Simon Greene and his friends laughed at Antonio when he went home, and the next morning they laughed at Antonio when he arrived at school with Ralph Robinson.

'What are you laughing at?' Ralph demanded.

'Haven't you heard?' said Simon Greene. 'Antonio wants people to sign up for a play he hasn't even chosen yet.'

'So?'

'*So?* Don't tell me *you're* in Antonio's wonderful play as well' said Simon Greene sneeringly.

'Maybe I am. Maybe I am!' Ralph declared. He turned to Antonio. 'Am I?'

'We'll have to see if there's a part for you,' said Antonio.

'He'll have to see if there's a part for you!' shouted Simon Greene after them as they walked away, and his loud friends laughed as if this were the funniest remark they had ever heard.

'How can there not be a part for me?' demanded Ralph when they had got away from Simon Greene. 'You haven't even chosen the play yet!'

'Casting actors is a serious business, Ralph,' said Antonio. 'You have to get the right person for the right part.'

'Well, in this case you'd better get the right part for the right person. You'd better get a part where someone has to eat a lot. That's what you'd better get!'

Antonio smiled to himself. He had found his first actor. After that, Ralph Robinson was the strongest defender of the play.

Antonio wondered if anyone else would dare come forward while there were so many jokes about him and his play flying around. All day long Simon Greene and the other great actors in the school mocked Antonio's idea. Who ever heard of getting together a cast without knowing which play you were going to perform? But that afternoon, when Antonio and Ralph were walking home from school through the park, they found Shoshi Vargaz waiting for them on one of the benches.

'Antonio,' said Shoshi as they came up to her. 'Are you putting on a play?'

'Of course he's putting on a play,' answered Ralph. 'Haven't you heard?'

'That's what I heard,' said Shoshi.

'Only he doesn't know what it is yet, understand?' Ralph said threateningly.

'Of course I understand.'

Antonio and Ralph could barely hear Shoshi. Shoshi hardly ever raised her voice above a whisper. She moved up along the bench. Antonio and Ralph sat next to her.

'Do you still need actors?' asked Shoshi in her soft voice.

'Yes,' said Antonio.

'Do you still need girl actors? I bet you've already got lots and lots.'

'We can still fit in an extra girl actor,' answered Ralph.

'Then, can I be in the play?' asked Shoshi.

'Yes,' said Antonio. 'You'd be perfect. You would be perfect, Shoshi.'

'Perfect,' said Ralph.

But afterwards Ralph asked: 'Why would Shoshi Vargaz be perfect?'

'Perfect for the part,' answered Antonio.

'Which part?'

'Shoshi's part.'

Ralph frowned. He said: 'Antonio, are you sure this is wise? The audience won't be able to hear Shoshi. No one can ever hear Shoshi. We couldn't hear her, and we were sitting right next to her.'

'That's why she would be perfect for the part. Only someone like Shoshi can play Shoshi's part.'

Ralph found it hard to argue with Antonio's logic. He found it hard to understand as well.

'You couldn't play Shoshi's part,' said Antonio.

'No,' said Ralph.

'And Shoshi couldn't play your part.'

Ralph laughed. Imagine Shoshi Vargaz trying to play his part!

The next day they got two more actors. One of them was a girl called Willi Brindle and the other was a boy called Paul Snee. Willi Brindle had flaming red hair and a voice as loud as Shoshi's voice was soft. When she whispered you could hear her in the next street. Paul Snee was as round as a ball and his face was as red as a tomato. He made excellent jokes and no one laughed at them more than he. Antonio said they were both perfect, perfect for their parts.

But still they didn't have a play. As the five of them left school that afternoon, Simon Greene and his friends laughed louder than ever.

'What are you going to do, make up your own play?' shouted Simon Greene.

'Maybe. Maybe we will,' replied Willi Brindle in a voice loud enough to blow the hair off their heads, and Paul Snee swaggered past on his short legs as if there were nothing simpler in the world.

Late that night, Antonio climbed the stairs to his mother's study. Professor Kettering was at her desk. When she was writing one of her medical books, Professor Kettering sometimes worked almost the whole night through and only took a short nap as the sun came up.

Antonio said: 'Mama, what plays are there?'

Professor Kettering smiled, putting down her pen.

'What do you mean, Antonio? There are all sorts of plays, hundreds of plays. More, much more. People have been writing plays since … people could write. Even longer.'

'How could people write plays before they could write?' objected Antonio.

'Well, with the first plays, they thought them up. This was long before people learned to write. By performing them, they passed them on from one generation to the next. Later, when people learned to write, they put them down on paper.'

'Which ones do you know?'

'Oh, Antonio. I couldn't say. There are so many.'

Antonio didn't know many plays, although he had seen lots of Scarrabo's magic performances. He had seen school pantomimes as well, but he knew that the acting in them wasn't very good. Once, Professor Kettering had taken him to see a play in a theatre. Antonio couldn't remember much about that play. It was very long and solemn and he fell asleep for part of it. There was an elderly man sitting on one side of him and he fell asleep as well. The only other plays Antonio knew were the ones he had been told about, the ones in which Theodore Guzman had starred, *Hamlet*, and the one about the horse and the manor, but Antonio really didn't know anything about those plays.

'How do you choose a play?' Antonio asked.

'I suppose ... you know something about it, and if you like the sound of it, you go,' said Professor Kettering.

'No, but if you were an actor, how would you choose a play to act in?'

'That would be much more difficult,' said Professor Kettering.

Scarrabo the Magnificent agreed. Walter Flood and Louisa Roberts were with him in the invention room, making sure everything was in order for his next show.

'Choosing a play—that is much more difficult,' Scarrabo said, polishing a set of chains. 'That is a matter of artistic judgement.'

Antonio thought about this carefully. Artistic judgement. How did one learn artistic judgement?

'It's the same with your father's tricks,' said Walter Flood, sharpening the blades of Scarrabo's throwing knives. 'Choosing a trick is a matter of artistic judgement as well. Which trick to perform? Which one to open the performance, which one to close it? These are perhaps the most important questions a magician has to answer. How many tricks are there in the world? A thousand? Five thousand?'

'More, Walter,' said Louisa Roberts.

'You see, Antonio, more than five thousand. And yet, in one performance, how many tricks can you perform? Twenty? Thirty? How do you decide which thirty you are going to use? And in what order? Artistic judgement. Listen to me, Antonio. When I was a youngster I was apprentice to a magician called Howard the Entertaining. In reality Howard was a very great magician. Your father won't mind me saying that I have never seen the Fishbowl Turnover Trick performed better. Would you agree, Scarrabo?'

Scarrabo nodded his head. So did Louisa Roberts.

'But Howard never succeeded. Never made it big, never got the crowds. Why? He had talent, that wasn't the problem. He was a wonderful magician, and he didn't get nervous. But he had no artistic judgement. For instance, he'd start his show with his biggest trick—after that, who was interested in the rest of the performance? People felt let down, even though they'd seen better tricks than they could see in any other show in town. No sense of suspense. And his name: Howard the Entertaining. What sort of a name is that for a magician? *Howard the Incredible*—yes. *Howard, Prince of Sorcerers*—yes. But Howard the Entertaining? No. Pitiful, that's what it was. Even when I was just an apprentice and we were sitting there after he'd finished a show in front of four people, I'd say to him: "Change it, Howard. Change the name." And what would he say? "My name is Howard and I'm entertaining. That's what I am and that's what I'm called." You see, Antonio, he lacked artistic judgement.'

The invention room was filled with the sound of polishing and scraping.

'But what if . . .' Antonio said slowly, 'what if you have artistic judgement, but you don't have the right trick? What if you have to use *another* trick?'

'Another trick?' repeated Scarrabo. 'Another trick?' he cried, turning to Walter Flood and Louisa Roberts.

Walter and Louisa shook their heads in disapproval.

'When you don't have the right trick—you invent!' roared Scarrabo the Magnificent. He dropped the chains with a crash, leapt to his feet, grabbed a pile of plates and began to juggle furiously, spinning round and round the room. 'You invent! You invent!' he roared again.

'That's the very best part,' added Louisa Roberts.

'But what about plays?' said Antonio.

'And *what* about plays?' cried Scarrabo, now juggling with one hand behind his back.

'You wouldn't invent plays,' said Antonio.

'And why not, I'd like to know?' demanded Scarrabo. 'Why not?'

Scarrabo hurled the plates up in a dazzling arc and caught them one after the other.

'Plays!' said Scarrabo, holding the plates out for Walter to take, breathing heavily. 'How do you think plays start life, Antonio? Do you think people dig them up; do you think they go fishing for them? People invent them, that's how. Anyone can do it. Your name doesn't have to be Goldblum or Butcher. If you need a play— invent! Artistic judgement, that's all it takes.'

Antonio called the first meeting of the actors. They met after school in the park near the duckpond.

'Is this a rehearsal?' asked Paul Snee.

'How can it be a rehearsal?' roared Willi Brindle. 'We haven't got a play yet.'

'We need a play,' whispered Shoshi Vargaz.

Ralph Robinson looked at Antonio. They had the actors, now they needed a play.

Antonio said: 'Does anyone know a play they want to perform?'

71

'We thought you were going to choose a play,' said Shoshi.

'That's right,' added Willi, 'you advertised.'

'The advertiser chooses the play,' said Paul.

'Well, I know one play,' said Antonio. 'It's called *Hamlet*. We can do that one.'

The others waited for Antonio to tell them more.

'It's not just any old play,' Antonio added hurriedly. 'It's about a prince whose uncle kills his father and then marries his mother, and then the ghost of his father comes back to the prince and tells him what happened.'

'And then?' asked Willi.

'I'm not sure exactly how it goes, but I could find out. Everyone dies in the end.'

'Everyone?' whispered Shoshi.

'Who wants to do a play about a dead king?' said Paul.

'And who believes in ghosts, anyway?' demanded Willi.

No one seemed very excited about the idea of doing *Hamlet*. Antonio didn't really want to do *Hamlet* either. Using artistic judgement, it didn't seem to be the right play. And they couldn't possibly do it as well as Mr Guzman, whose performance was the last word on the matter. But he would have to get a play from somewhere. None of his actors looked very happy. It looked as if some of them might give up the whole idea if they

72

didn't get a play soon. And not just any old play, full of dead kings and ghosts.

'What *I* want to do,' said Willi Brindle suddenly, in a voice that made half the ducks on the pond take to the air in fright, 'is a play about a girl. About a girl with such a wonderful loud voice that she becomes the greatest singer in the world.'

'And just who would this girl be?' asked Ralph knowingly.

'Just a girl,' said Willi.

Ralph snorted. 'Who wants to do a play about a girl with a loud voice?'

'Well, Mr Robinson, if you're so clever what would *you* do?'

'That's up to Antonio. But if I was choosing, I would do a play about a boy who could eat so much he became the greatest food taster in the world.'

'Hah!'

'Oh, yes,' said Ralph. 'People don't know how important food tasters are. Every restaurant needs one, for instance. And every president needs one. Have you thought about that? Imagine, dishing up food to a president that might only be half cooked! People don't appreciate food tasters, that's half the trouble with the world.'

Antonio laughed. Everyone laughed. Ralph folded his arms across his chest and almost smiled himself.

'What would you do, Paul?' Antonio asked.

Paul Snee's red face went even redder than usual. 'Oh, I don't know,' he said.

'Come on, Paul,' demanded Willi, 'what would you do?'

'Well, if I had to choose,' said Paul, 'I would do a play about a short boy who told jokes, who told such good jokes that people stopped laughing at him because of how short he was and just listened to the jokes he told.'

'And?' said Willi.

'And . . . ' Paul thought. 'Well, because this boy was also a bit too fat and everyone kept telling him he couldn't eat everything he liked, I might borrow the great food taster from Ralph's play and let him eat half of everything that was prepared for the great comedian.'

'But the food taster would need to eat more than half the comedian's food,' said Ralph, waving a finger in the air. 'The food taster has a great appetite. That's what makes him such a good food taster.'

'Then he could taste the food for the great singer from Willi's play as well,' said Paul.

'*If* she let him,' said Willi.

Ralph gave Willi a harsh stare. 'She'd better let him, if she knows what's good for her.'

Willi tossed her head, throwing back her flaming red hair.

'What about you, Shoshi,' said Antonio, 'what play would you do?'

'I would do a play . . .' said Shoshi.

Everyone leaned towards Shoshi, straining to hear her over the honking of the ducks on the pond.

'I would do a play . . .' said Shoshi.

'Louder, Shoshi!' said Ralph.

'No,' said Shoshi. 'You listen harder for a change. I would do a play about a girl who can't talk, and who everyone ignores. She just sits at her desk near the wall. This girl just sits at her desk beside the wall even at lunchtime, when everyone else is playing outside. But although she can't talk she writes wonderful poems that everyone loves to read.'

Shoshi looked down at the grass.

'Only they don't know that the girl who can't talk is the one who writes the poems,' she added.

'If the girl who can't talk wrote wonderful songs instead of wonderful poems, she could give them to the great singer from Willi's play to sing them,' said Paul.

'That's true. A lot of the poems are almost songs any-way,' said Shoshi.

'And since the great food taster is already tasting the great singer's food, he would have to taste the great songwriter's food as well,' said Ralph. 'And the great songwriter, being so small and quiet, would have the appetite of a sparrow, so the great food taster would probably have to eat three quarters of her food—at least!'

'Possibly,' said Shoshi.

Everyone laughed at Ralph again. He didn't take offence. He was very happy with himself, since he had managed to get a job tasting food for no fewer than three people.

Then Shoshi said: 'What about you, Antonio? What play would you do?'

'Me?' Antonio thought. 'I would do a play about someone who puts on a play. He puts on a play because it's the only way to do something really special.'

Ralph frowned.

'I don't understand,' said Willi.

Antonio shrugged. 'That's the play I would put on. A play about someone who puts on a play. And it would be a new play because there isn't an old play that is just right in his artistic judgement.'

Shoshi said: 'But there isn't such a play, is there?'

'No. And there isn't a play with a loud singer and a hungry food taster and a dieting comedian and a silent songwriter.'

Antonio lay right back on the grass and looked up at the sky. A duck dipped swiftly through the air above him.

'At least, there isn't yet,' said Antonio. 'But there could be.'

He sat bolt upright.

'There could be, if we want there to be. When you don't have a play, invent. Invent!' he exclaimed, feeling just as if he were Scarrabo the Magnificent juggling plates around and around the invention room.

'A new play?' said Willi doubtfully.

'Why not?' said Antonio. 'Otherwise we'll have to use an old play. Something about kings and ghosts.'

'And where will we perform this new play?' asked Paul.

'Where?'

Antonio looked around. Above the top of the trees, he could see the square tower of Duke's House.

'On the lawn in front of the Duke's House, of course,' he replied.

'On the lawn?' said Willi.

'On the lawn,' said Ralph, with a big grin on his face. 'Where else?'

'And what do you think we'll call this play?' demanded Willi.

'*Four Stories*!' answered Antonio immediately. 'That's what it is, isn't it?'

'But what about your story?'

'My story is the play itself. My story is putting the play on.'

'And what will we call *ourselves*?' whispered Shoshi.

Antonio thought. 'The Dolphin Theatre,' he said, imagining the most beautiful fountain in the courtyard of the great house.

'Yes,' murmured Shoshi. 'The Dolphin Theatre.'

'And there's one more thing we'll need,' said Antonio. 'We'll need a poster to announce our play.'

A poster that everyone would see, even Mr Guzman, even if he only happened to look out once from behind his lace curtains.

CHAPTER 9

The poster had gold letters on a red background, just like the poster that Antonio had seen on Mr Guzman's wall. Paul Snee got the paints for it from his uncle, who owned a paint shop in the city. Shoshi Vargaz, who was the best of them at drawing, painted it. She painted five posters. Ralph Robinson took two and Willi Brindle took two and they each put one up at school and Ralph nailed his second one to a tree beside the playground in the park and Willi stuck her second one to a wall in the fruit market where her parents had a stall selling pineapples, mangoes and roasted nuts.

Antonio took the fifth poster. He asked Mr Carman where he could put it.

Mr Carman read the poster. 'Am I invited?' he asked.

'Of course,' said Antonio.

'Then you can stick it on the railing of the main stair-case.'

'I don't think the railing of the main staircase is a good place for it,' said Antonio.

'Why not?' inquired Mr Carman.

'Some people never go upstairs. If they live on the ground floor, for instance, they never go upstairs.'

'But they all look up at the railing.'

'Some people don't.'

'Who?'

'People who just come out for a walk and don't look around very much. I want to put it in a place where *everyone* will see it.'

'Well, you can stick it on the wall under the archway. Even people who don't look around very much would see it there.'

Antonio shook his head.

'Why not, Antonio?'

'Some people hardly even come out. They might not get to the archway.'

'Antonio,' said Mr Carman, 'where *do* you want to put it?'

Antonio pointed to the wall directly opposite Mr Guzman's window.

Mr Carman smiled. 'All right. Just be sure to take it down after Saturday.'

But the posters weren't painted and weren't put up for nearly a fortnight after the five actors decided to perform the new play called *Four Stories*. First of all they had to invent it. This wasn't so easy. How do you take four stories and make them into one play?

Willi Brindle said they had to have everything written down. She said that it would be their script. When they met beside the duckpond two days later she brought a pad and a pen and got ready to write. They all sat in a circle and then they argued for an hour and by the end of it they hadn't even agreed on the first line of the play. They wasted the whole afternoon. Paul Snee, who was good at maths, calculated that if they kept going at that rate it would take seventeen years to finish the play. They might finish it in fifteen years if they agreed to meet during the summer holidays.

So they decided that they wouldn't write it down. How could they all tell what Shoshi Vargaz, for instance, had to say? Only Shoshi could decide that.

Antonio tried to imagine the atmosphere in Scarrabo's invention room when he and Walter Flood and Louisa

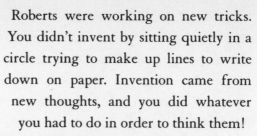

Roberts were working on new tricks. You didn't invent by sitting quietly in a circle trying to make up lines to write down on paper. Invention came from new thoughts, and you did whatever you had to do in order to think them!

When they met the next day, the first thing Antonio did was stand on his head. The others thought he was crazy. But some very interesting ideas came into his head with all the blood that rushed there from his legs. Then Antonio got up and juggled three stones while weaving in and out amongst the others. They thought he was even crazier. But Antonio got them to tell their stories, one by one, as he juggled, and they watched him, laughing, and talked about their ideas, the stories about the girl with the loud voice and the boy with the big appetite and the boy who told jokes and the silent girl who wrote songs. Each one spoke, and maybe it was the fact that they didn't have to worry about writing everything down, or maybe it was the sight of Antonio juggling like a madman, but whatever it was they came out with four stories that were worth listening to.

Antonio said: 'Those are the stories. Now we have to put them together. Can you juggle?'

None of them could. Not even Ralph Robinson, who had seen Scarrabo the Magnificent juggling on the lawn hundreds of times.

'Anyone can juggle,' he said. 'I'll teach you.'

Shoshi was the quickest to learn. It was as if juggling were natural for her, like turning a somersault or riding a bicycle. It made Ralph and Paul mad, but they couldn't compete. Soon she was tossing four stones with ease while they were still struggling with three. Willi found it hardest of all.

'Don't worry,' said Antonio. 'Use two stones instead of three.'

'That's not juggling,' objected Ralph.

'It is for Willi,' replied Antonio.

They spent the rest of the meeting learning to juggle. Antonio knew they must look silly, throwing stones in the air and making mistakes and once or twice even hitting each other on the head. Simon Greene and his friends, who had turned up on the other side of

the duckpond, pointed and laughed. They pretended to juggle as well, throwing their arms around and staggering as if they were drunk. Antonio didn't care. He kept juggling and so did the others, even Willi. They had four separate stories, and now they had to put them together into one play. That was going to take a lot of invention. And as far as Antonio knew, the best way to invent was to juggle.

The next time they met, Antonio brought a basket full of spongy juggling balls from Scarrabo's invention room.

'Come on,' he said. 'What are you waiting for?'

For a while there was only the sound of juggling balls slapping in and out of hands. There was the sound of balls slapping on the ground quite a lot as well. Everyone was concentrating.

Finally Antonio began, still juggling as he spoke.

'The first scene is a boy who has a great appetite. He is complaining that he never gets enough to eat.'

'Complaining bitterly,' said Ralph at once, his eyes on the balls rising and falling in front of him. 'In fact, in the very first scene he has to eat something, to show what an appetite he has.'

'And there is a small, thin girl, who can't speak,' Antonio continued, tossing the balls higher and higher. 'She's sitting near the boy who can't get enough to eat.'

'Why is she sitting there?' asked Ralph.

'She's his sister,' whispered Shoshi.

Ralph dropped his juggling balls. 'Is she?'

'Yes,' said Antonio.

They heard laughter from the other side of the duck-pond as Ralph bent down to pick up the balls. Simon Greene and his friends had come to make fun again. Ralph glanced at them and threw a ball into the air.

'The girl offers to let her brother taste her food if he will sing her songs for her,' said Shoshi.

'Why?' demanded Ralph, messing up his juggling again. 'Why should he sing them for her?'

'Because she can't sing them herself,' roared Willi in frustration, glaring at the boys on the other side of the pond. She was having a terrible time trying to toss two balls from hand to hand.

'She can't sing them herself,' repeated Antonio, ignoring the shouts from Simon Greene and his friends. 'She can't talk, remember? So when she makes the offer to the boy with the enormous appetite she must write it—because she has to write everything she wants to say, or use sign language—and he reads it out, so the audience knows what's happening.'

'But I can tell you, the boy with the enormous appetite doesn't want to sing,' said Ralph. 'He hates singing. He hates it so much it isn't even worth the extra food.'

'Exactly,' said Paul Snee, whose juggling was becoming better and better, 'but what if he knows a girl with a loud voice who loves singing? What if he knows she'll want the songs?'

'Why doesn't the silent girl just take the songs to the girl with the loud voice herself?' objected Ralph.

'Because she doesn't know her,' replied Paul. He stopped juggling for a moment. 'They don't know each other, Ralph, what other reason could there be?'

Ralph thought about it. He nodded.

'And in the second scene he offers the songs to the girl with the loud voice,' said Antonio, 'if she will—'

'—let him taste her food!' cried Ralph, who could finally see that these songs were worth not one extra portion of food, but two.

They laughed. Then no one said anything.

'The boy with the enormous appetite, he mustn't let the silent girl know that the loud girl will sing her songs,' Antonio suggested. 'That's the key. He mustn't let his sister go with him. Otherwise, the first girl will give them directly to the second girl and he won't get anything at all.'

Everyone was juggling and thinking, trying to ignore the boys on the other side of the duckpond. How did they go on from there?

'Well, let's say the boy with the enormous appetite has a friend,' Paul said eventually, still thinking as he spoke.

'A friend?'

'Yes,' said Paul. 'A friend who tells excellent jokes. But this friend never gets the chance to tell them to an audience. So the boy with the enormous appetite, he asks the friend to keep the silent girl busy while he takes the songs to the loud girl. And of course, the friend thinks this is great.'

'Because he'll get to tell his jokes to the silent girl, who'll be his audience,' said Antonio.

'Exactly. So there'll have to be a scene between the first two scenes where the boy with the big appetite goes to get his friend, before he goes off to the girl with the loud voice.'

'And the boy keeps her busy with his jokes. Five jokes, six jokes, one after the other,' said Antonio.

'Then that's another scene as well,' whispered Shoshi. 'The silent girl listens to the funny boy's jokes, and she laughs silently.'

'Exactly,' said Paul. 'That's four scenes so far. But

wait! Listen to this: what if the boy with the enormous appetite didn't tell the boy with the jokes that the song-writer doesn't talk? Then he'll think she's not laughing at all!'

'So?' said Ralph.

'So it would make him angry,' whispered Shoshi.

'Right. It would make any comedian angry,' said Paul. 'So what does he do? He goes off to look for the boy with the enormous appetite to tell him what he thinks of his sister.'

'And he finds him just as he begins to sample the loud girl's food, to make sure it's worth the songs he is giving her,' said Ralph.

'Right,' said Paul Snee.

'But now ... Well, can't the boy who tells jokes see what's going on?' said Willi.

'Of course not,' said Ralph.

'Yes he can. He can see everything, Ralph Robinson. He can see that the girl with the loud voice is going to have a concert with the songs, and he'll want to tell his jokes at the concert as well.'

'Exactly, Willi,' said Paul. 'If the girl with the loud voice is going to have a concert, why shouldn't he have a chance to tell the audience his jokes?'

Antonio was nodding. 'And in the next scene, the boy who tells jokes says to the boy with the big appetite that if he doesn't get to tell his jokes at the concert, then he'll tell the silent girl who the singer is, and then the boy with the big appetite won't be needed at all!'

'But in the scene after that,' said Willi, 'when the boy with the big appetite goes back to tell the girl with the loud voice that there will have to be a few jokes at her concert, she tells him that she won't stand for it. No jokes! On no account. She doesn't want them at all.'

'Ralph,' Antonio said, 'you're in big trouble!'

The others laughed. Everyone had stopped juggling and was looking at Ralph.

Ralph put his hands on his hips. 'Nothing I can't handle!' he said.

They continued juggling and inventing the scenes for the play. They forgot all about Simon Greene and his friends and didn't even notice that they had got bored and disappeared. Each one added ideas, and somehow it all came together, the four separate stories became entwined and woven together in one thick strand that you couldn't pick apart. Another thing that happened was that the play got more complicated as they invented it. It was a surprise to all of them; they thought it would be quite simple. But the character that joined them all together was the boy with the big appetite, who rushed around trying to keep everyone from knowing what the others were doing, and every time he said or did something it complicated everything that he had said and done already. In the end, of course, everyone did find out what was going on and the boy with the big appetite lost out on his food tasting altogether.

'Maybe you should have told the silent girl the truth at the start,' Shoshi told Ralph. 'Maybe she would have let you have some of her food anyway.'

Ralph shrugged. 'A boy with an appetite like that has to try for the maximum, Shoshi.'

In the end the play had fourteen scenes and in the last scene there was a concert at which the loud girl finally sang the silent girl's songs and the funny boy told his funniest jokes. The boy with the enormous appetite missed the show completely. That was the last scene in the original version.

But then Ralph said that the ending wasn't quite right in his opinion and he said they should add a fifteenth scene where the boy with the big appetite, who was so unhappy at having lost all that food tasting, went to a restaurant to try to cheer himself up. And at the restaurant he would eat three hamburgers washed down with two milkshakes and followed by three pieces of pie. Ralph gave the numbers exactly. It was the perfect size for a meal on such an occasion, neither too large nor too small. And meanwhile, as he was eating all this food, the chef of the restaurant would creep out of the kitchen to watch and he would be so amazed by the boy's appetite that he would offer him a job tasting food in the kitchen.

Everyone listened to Ralph's ending. Shoshi wasn't

sure, Willi thought it was funny, Paul Snee didn't like it. Antonio thought about it for a long time. They took a vote. Ralph's idea won three to two, and they agreed to keep it.

Then Shoshi asked: 'But what about you, Antonio? What about your story?'

'My story is the play,' said Antonio. 'I don't need to be in it.'

'But you *have* to be in it!' cried Willi and Paul together.

'Then I'll be the chef in Ralph's restaurant scene. I'll be in it at the end,' replied Antonio. 'And of course I'll arrange the chairs and things between the scenes. Someone has to do that.'

'But there's one other problem,' said Willi. 'What about the songs I'm supposed to sing. Where will we get them?'

'Don't worry,' said Shoshi, 'I've got them already.'

Altogether, they met eight times
before they got everything right.
After they invented the outline
they had to fill in the details.
Once there was a spring shower
and they all ran to the bandstand
on the other side of the park, where
they continued the meeting. They went
over each part and tried to work out what they would do

and say in each scene. They gave each other ideas. They didn't try to write anything down or make everything fixed. The lines came out a little differently each time they practised. Antonio thought, that's the idea of practising, to find the best lines.

Not everything went smoothly. There were differences of opinion. Sometimes, when they were stuck, Antonio juggled some stones until he thought of an idea. Shoshi often juggled as well. Slowly each line and part of the play took shape in their minds.

The last meeting they had was almost like a rehearsal. It was a good meeting. At the end of it Antonio thought, this play isn't going to be bad. This play is going to be something special, maybe even special enough for Mr Guzman.

But Simon Greene and his friends didn't agree. When they saw the posters for the play at school, they laughed louder than ever.

'So this is the play?' Simon Greene shouted. 'Who's it by? What's it called?'

'*Four Stories*,' answered Willi Brindle, who could out-shout Simon Greene three times over. 'Can't you read?'

'Four jugglers, you mean. We've all seen you by the duckpond. Why don't you put on your play in a circus?'

'Why don't you come on Saturday and see it?' replied Antonio S.

CHAPTER 10

Simon Greene did come on Saturday to see the play. So did his friends. They arrived early and sat down in a bunch on the lawn and even from a distance you could see they had only come to laugh and sneer.

One of Simon Greene's friends said very loudly, so that everyone would hear: 'They don't even have a stage!'

It was true, there was no stage. There was only the lawn in front of Duke's House, which Mr Carman had mown for them the day before. The only furniture was a table and a few chairs from the Robinsons' apartment. And as costumes, they had decided, they were going to wear their normal clothes. Only Willi Brindle, who wanted to wear something special when she gave the concert with Shoshi's songs, had a new green jacket that her mother had bought for her.

At three o'clock on Saturday afternoon Antonio went out onto the lawn and measured out a big rectangle of grass, twenty paces long and twelve paces wide, and he marked it off with white stones that he had collected in a bucket the day before. The grass inside the rectangle was where the actors would act. Then Antonio went and got Ralph Robinson and they brought down the chairs from his apartment. Two of Ralph's brothers helped them with the table. They put the furniture a little way from one edge of the stage, so that Antonio could drag the pieces on and off as they were needed. The actors who were off stage would sit quietly among the chairs while the others acted.

After that there was only one piece of equipment missing: the hamper containing the food that Ralph had to eat in the various scenes. Shoshi was responsible for bringing it and in Ralph's opinion it was the most important piece of equipment for the play, much more important than tables and chairs. As he said over and over again, you can sit on the ground but you can't eat fresh air. Ralph had managed to make sure that he sampled something in almost every scene in which he appeared. He had been very careful to specify exactly what each dish was and everyone's mother had spent the morning cooking something for him. Ralph's own mother had made the hamburgers, milkshakes and pie for the restaurant scene at the end. He wouldn't trust anyone else to make these important items.

It was after four o'clock when Shoshi arrived. Ralph heaved a sigh of relief and went over to inspect the food. 'It's all cold,' Shoshi whispered to him as she put down the covered hamper. 'You poor boy. You have to eat it all cold.'

Ralph grinned happily. Cold or hot, it made no difference to him.

Then Willi Brindle arrived in her new green jacket, and Paul Snee came. By now it was half past four. The Dolphin Theatre was ready for action.

Paul and Willi went over to have a look at the stage and when they came back Willi asked if the stage was big enough and Antonio said that he thought it was. Paul asked Shoshi if she had brought the food and Shoshi said that she had. Then they were quiet. Nobody had anything to say. There were still twenty minutes to wait and there was nothing for them to do except stand around and watch the people coming over to sit on the lawn in front of the stage. And watching the audience arrive just made them feel more nervous than they already were.

Paul cracked one of his jokes and they all laughed and then they were all quiet again.

Simon Greene and his loud friends had arrived. Paul's father came over the lawn, together with the uncle and aunt who owned the paint shop in the city. Four of Paul's cousins came as well, and they all sat together on a big rug. Shoshi's parents and brother had come with her when she brought the hamper. Some friends from school arrived. Willi's parents couldn't come, but the fishmonger who owned the stall next to them in the market had said that he would come instead, and Antonio recognised him as he sat down on the grass.

For a moment Antonio wished he could walk across the grass and sit down next to the fishmonger as well, instead of standing there in front of all those watching eyes.

At five minutes to five Scarrabo the Magnificent came out, together with Walter Flood and Louisa Roberts. A minute later Professor Kettering hurried out to join them.

Ralph's mother came out of the house, carrying baby Rhonda. Ralph's brothers followed close behind.

Antonio looked at his watch. It was five o'clock exactly. There were more than thirty people in front of the stage, sitting on rugs, or chairs or on the grass.

Everything was ready.

Antonio looked back at the house. A figure came out of the entrance. Was it Mr Guzman at last? No, it didn't look anything like him. It was Mr Carman.

Antonio looked at his watch again. Two minutes past five. All over the lawn people were waiting, gazing at the actors.

'Come on, Antonio, what are you waiting for?' whispered Ralph.

'Just another minute.'

'Why?'

'We're still waiting for someone.'

Willi gave him an impatient look. 'Who?'

'Just one more minute.'

Where was Mr Guzman? He always walked so slowly, maybe he was still on his way.

No one else appeared. Willi poked Antonio in the ribs.

It was five past five. Mr Guzman wasn't coming. The poster had been perfectly clear. The play was to begin at five o'clock.

Antonio threw one last glance at the empty entrance to the house. He couldn't delay any longer. He stepped over the line of pebbles and onto the stage. He looked around at the audience, but he didn't start speaking straight away. It was so quiet. So many faces were looking at him.

He held out his hands. 'Welcome to the Duke's House,' he said loudly.

In the silence, the sound of his own voice almost took him by surprise.

'This afternoon the Dolphin Theatre presents a new play called *Four Stories*.'

That was all he said. He stepped off the stage, brought out one chair, put it in place and stepped back again. Shoshi and Ralph came on. Shoshi sat on the ground with her feet curled up beneath her. Ralph sat slouched on the chair.

For a moment, they just sat there. You could hear the faint honking of the ducks all the way from the park. Then Ralph turned his head and said, 'I'm hungry. I'm terribly, *teeerribly* hungry. And it's still three hours to dinnertime!'

CHAPTER 11

There were certain problems with the
play. For a start, someone must have told
Willi Brindle that actors always have to
speak extra loudly in order to be heard,
and she shouted every line. Being on
the stage with her was like standing
next to someone using a megaphone.
And she always looked at the audience,
never at the person she was talking to.
Maybe someone had told her that actors
have to do that as well.

Another problem was that Paul Snee got nervous
and began to forget some of the things he was meant to
say. He even forgot some of his jokes. That made him
angry and then he forgot even more things. Antonio
whispered to him and tried to calm him down when
he was standing at the side between scenes, but every
time he went back onto the stage he got nervous and
forgot something and then it started all over again. It
was surprising. Normally Paul Snee didn't have any
trouble telling jokes.

There was something else that made Paul angry. It turned out that the actor who got the biggest laughs from the audience was not him with his jokes, but Ralph Robinson. This was not something they had planned, it was something that came out of the play itself. Everything that had seemed so serious and complicated when they invented it became funny when Ralph acted it. He became the star of the show. There was only one thing Ralph cared about in the play, food, and people giggled and grinned at his never-ending search for it. Antonio found himself laughing as well. The longer the play went on the funnier Ralph became. And something else happened. You couldn't say exactly when Ralph started to do it, but after a while he began to make it funnier, not by cracking jokes, but by being more and more serious, more and more demanding in his search for food. Antonio could see he was doing it on purpose. By now people were laughing even before Ralph opened his mouth to talk. It was as if Ralph were changing as he acted, fitting himself to the part. Or maybe the part was taking him over.

Something similar happened to the others as well. They were acting the parts they had invented by the duckpond, but somehow the parts weren't exactly the same as the ones they had invented. Shoshi Vargaz wasn't just a silent songwriter. As the play went on she became somehow sadder, even tragic, and it was almost as if her silences began to speak. Willi Brindle wasn't just a loud girl, she was the world's loudest girl, especially because of her idea that she had to shout all the time. And Paul Snee, who was getting nervous and angry, began telling his jokes angrily. He wasn't just a comedian, he was an angry comedian. Antonio was fascinated by the effect the play was having. It was as if he were watching real people out there on the stage, real stories—and not just the stories they had imagined beside the duckpond, but different stories. These weren't the same four people he had juggled with beside the duckpond. They were, but they weren't.

Maybe the audience was fascinated as well. There were moments, when Shoshi was just sitting there with her feet tucked up under her, responding with her eyes to something Ralph had said, when the silence on the lawn in front of Duke's House was so heavy that you could almost feel its weight. People didn't laugh when Paul forgot a line, they sensed his anger. Sometimes Antonio looked out at the audience on the lawn. Everyone was watching the actors. They weren't aware of him gazing at them. Even Simon Greene was staring at the stage.

That was how Antonio discovered that Mr Guzman had arrived.

He didn't know exactly when Mr Guzman had appeared. But halfway through the play Antonio turned to look at the audience and there he was, in his Homburg hat, not sitting on the lawn, but standing, resting his weight on a cane. Just like everyone else, he was gazing attentively at the actors.

They were coming to the end of the play. Antonio carried a chair onto the stage. Ralph waited with him at the side. This was the scene when Shoshi and Willi and Paul worked out all the tricks he had been playing and decided to leave him out of things. As they were talking, Antonio glanced at Ralph. He was watching the other three with narrowed eyes. Antonio could tell: at that moment Ralph wasn't acting. He was feeling it, really feeling it, as if three friends of his were really cutting him out of something.

Then there was the scene of the concert. Paul told four of his jokes and finally managed to get a couple of punch lines out, and then Willi sang one of Shoshi's songs. At this point, the way they had invented the play, only Willi was meant to be on the stage. But the scene changed. Shoshi stayed there as well, curled up silently in a corner of the stage, as Willi sang her song.

The song was about a fish who swims in a harbour during the day but each night goes far, far out to sea. Antonio thought that Willi sang it too loudly. But he was watching Shoshi. Everyone on the lawn was listening to Willi but watching Shoshi. And Shoshi, who had simply decided to sit like that on the stage even though it was wasn't planned, wasn't facing the audience. She wasn't watching Willi sing in her loud voice. She was turned to the side, staring silently across the lawn, and people could only see the side of her face.

Then it was the last scene. The table went on. The hamburgers and milkshakes and pieces of pie were piled up. Ralph Robinson sat himself down.

Ralph stared at the food in front of him. He sighed. He picked up the first hamburger and gazed lovingly at it, the way a boy with an enormous appetite would do if had just lost his job as food taster for three people. The audience giggled. Ralph ate the first hamburger slowly. He picked the second one up. He spent a little less time gazing at it, a little less time eating it. He simply stuffed the third one into his mouth. The audience was laughing. Antonio had stepped quietly onto the stage behind him, as if he were a chef creeping out of his kitchen to watch a champion eater in his restaurant. Each time Ralph put a piece of hamburger in his mouth, Antonio crept nearer. Each time he put a piece of pie in his mouth, Antonio peered closer. When Ralph drained the last milkshake and leaned back with his hands resting on his belly, Antonio straightened up, put his hands on his hips, and said: 'We need a food taster in this restaurant. I don't suppose you know where we could find one?'

Ralph looked at the audience. He gave them a secret grin. Then he turned around as if he had not even known that Antonio was there.

He waited a fraction of a moment longer.

'I think I know just who you need.'

That was the end of the play. Ralph and Antonio left the stage. The audience applauded. Paul and Willi and Shoshi and Ralph stepped back onto the grass stage, and Antonio joined them, and they bowed to the audience. Antonio stepped back to let the others, who had done almost all the acting, bow again. Antonio felt strangely happy. In front of him were Paul and Willi and Shoshi and Ralph. Beyond them was the audience. Everyone was smiling. Antonio felt as if he had done something— as if they had all done something—that wasn't just something you do everyday. He felt as if he had done something special.

He was smiling as well. He could see Scarrabo the Magnificent and Walter Flood and Louisa Roberts and Professor Kettering clapping. He looked for Mr Guzman. But the place where the Homburger had been standing was empty. Mr Guzman was already making his way back to the great house.

Antonio watched him. Mr Guzman had almost reached the entrance of the house. As Antonio looked, he stopped and turned around. He hooked his cane over his arm. Antonio did not take his eyes off him. He had the feeling that Mr Guzman was searching for him, that he wanted to be sure that Antonio was watching.

Mr Guzman clapped. He clapped three times exactly. Through the rest of the applause, Antonio could hear each one as clearly as if Mr Guzman were standing right in front of him.

Then Mr Guzman turned into the archway of the great house and disappeared.

CHAPTER 12

When Antonio S met Simon Greene at school on Monday, they found themselves just looking at each other for a moment, as if each was not sure what the other was going to say. This time, Simon Greene wasn't surrounded by his loud friends. The look Simon had on his face was almost a frown, as if he were struggling with something that was troubling him.

Simon Greene said: 'I was at your play on Saturday.'

'I know,' said Antonio, 'I saw you there. I'm sorry there wasn't any juggling for you. I know you were looking forward to that.'

Simon bit his lip. He looked as if he felt foolish. But for some reason he didn't come out and say, 'I'm sorry, I was foolish.' Antonio thought he would probably feel better if he did.

He said: 'I would like to see that play.'

'You've seen it,' said Antonio.

'No, I mean, I would like to *see* it. You know, the play, the script.'

'There's no such thing,' said Antonio.

Simon Greene looked as if he didn't believe him.

'It was good, Antonio. All right? It's got potential. Of course, it could be improved. Maybe you could work on it with me.'

The trouble with Simon Greene was that even now he still spoke as if Antonio would be lucky to have Simon working on *his* play.

'I'm not planning to work on it,' said Antonio.

'I'd like to see it,' Simon repeated.

'There's no such thing.'

Simon Greene put his hands in his pockets. He leaned against the school fence. 'Why not?'

Antonio shrugged. 'Because there isn't.'

'Then why don't you write it down now?'

'I don't know it all. I can't remember the lines everyone made up.'

'Then why don't you get the others and write it down together?' demanded Simon Greene.

'I don't think they could remember every line they made up.'

'Then they could make them up again!' Simon Greene looked angry. He shook his head, as if something were wrong. 'If you don't write it down now, you'll forget it. The longer you leave it the more you'll forget.'

Simon Greene was right. Something like that, like the lines people make up when they're acting, go right out of your head.

'You'll never be able to put it on again,' he said

harshly. 'It'll be gone forever, won't it?'

'Yes,' said Antonio.

'That's not what plays are for. Plays are for people to be able to see over and over, so they can see what other people think, the way other people live.'

'That's what you think.'

'Well, what do you think they're for?' demanded Simon Greene.

'I don't know what every play is for. Maybe some plays are for one thing and others have a different reason.'

Simon Greene didn't say anything to that. He stood there a moment longer. Finally he shook his head and walked away without saying another word.

Antonio watched him go. Simon Greene thought he was right. Nothing you could say would convince him that anyone knew more than him about plays. But Antonio didn't want to write down the script of *Four Stories* and he certainly didn't want to work on it with Simon Greene. That wasn't what the play was for.

But what *was* the play for? Mr Guzman had come out to see it. He had even applauded, but then he had simply disappeared again. Every time Antonio came down the stairs of the great house he expected to see Mr Guzman come out to talk to him, but the days and weeks went by and not once did the blue door of his apartment open. All the work and the effort, the juggling and the invention, turned out to be no more effective than knocking on the Homburger's door.

Everyone else thought the play had been a great success. Willi Brindle got a part singing in the school pantomime, although the Art teacher, who was the director, had to keep telling her to lower her voice. Paul Snee decided that stories about people were more interesting than jokes and the English teacher agreed to teach him how to write them. Shoshi Vargaz began sending her poems to the school magazine, and everyone said that they were the best poems that the magazine had ever printed. And as for Ralph Robinson, he had come to a major decision. Instead of being a food taster when he grew up, he was going to be a humorous actor.

'Antonio,' he said, 'it was such great fun to make everybody laugh.'

'People always laugh at you, Ralph.'

'No, this time I made them laugh on purpose. By the end of the play I knew just what I had to do. Do you remember the last scene? I knew that I had to wait just that one second more, just that extra tiny moment, before I answered you. Don't ask me how I knew, I just did. If I waited that extra *teensy-weensy* little second, it would be so much funnier. And I was right, wasn't I?'

He was. Even Scarrabo the Magnificent, who knew all there was to know about suspense, said that Ralph had a natural sense of timing.

Now Ralph spent all his spare time watching funny movies. He was trying to learn, he told Antonio. You don't become a humorous actor just by luck. You have to watch the experts.

'You didn't have to watch any experts to become a champion eater,' Antonio pointed out. 'You did that all by yourself.'

'True,' said Ralph, 'but this is different.'

Maybe Ralph was right. Both Scarrabo the Magnificent and Professor Kettering had learned by watching experts.

Yet for Antonio, nothing seemed to happen. Soon a week had gone by, and then a month, and then two months. Mr Guzman never even came out of his apartment. School finished for the year and Scarrabo the Magnificent and Professor Kettering took Antonio to the sea for a fortnight. They never stayed away any longer because the hospital couldn't spare Professor Kettering for more than two weeks. When they came back, Scarrabo was due to give his summer season of outdoor performances.

Scarrabo's summer season lasted a month and each performance was held in a different place in the city. He did an evening of magic tricks in Cobbler's Square and an afternoon of escapes from the cages in the old part of the zoo where the tigers used to be locked up. He did a twilight performance in the Solga Cave outside the city, which was one of his most unusual performances and was always incredibly popular. The vast cave was packed from two in the afternoon with people waiting for it to begin. As the sun went down Scarrabo performed feats with lights, and the effect of the flickering shadows on the walls of the cave was really something to be seen. Antonio never missed it. Each year he saw tricks he had never seen before and there were times when Scarrabo made up new sequences on the spot. Even Professor Kettering found time to go to the Solga Cave, and afterwards they all drove back together in Walter Flood's car.

By the time Scarrabo's summer season was drawing to an end, Antonio had given up hope of ever meeting Mr Guzman. It was months since the Dolphin Theatre had performed in front of Duke's House, and even longer since he had first peered through the crack and seen the poster hanging in Mr Guzman's room. It was obvious that the play was not good enough to impress the old Homburger, who had been such a great actor, and Antonio had even begun to feel foolish for ever imagining that it would. The three claps that Mr Guzman had given were probably only out of politeness. Antonio no longer looked expectantly at the Homburger's door, or imagined that Mr Guzman might be coming out to talk to him, when he came down the stairs to the courtyard of the great house.

Scarrabo's last performance of the outdoor season was always a Pendulum Escape from the old suspension bridge. This was the highest bridge over the river and the winds that blew beneath it were known for their rapid changes in direction. Never had Antonio seen the potato sack containing Scarrabo swing so high. The wind caught it and soon the sack was veering wildly in the swirling currents. Never had Antonio waited so long for Scarrabo to appear. The crowd held its breath. When Scarrabo finally emerged from the sack, the crowd was cheering even before he completed his somersaulting dive into the river.

After that, Scarrabo could relax. The summer season was over and there were no performances. Louisa Roberts went on vacation to the country and wasn't seen at Duke's House for almost three weeks. Walter Flood, who never took a holiday, didn't turn up to the invention room until midday, and spent most of his time reading books on great magicians of the past. In the warm summer evenings, after Professor Kettering came home from the hospital, they would sometimes borrow deckchairs from Mr Carman and sit on the lawn in front of the great house with a jug of iced tea and a chess set.

Walter Flood and Professor Kettering were both fine chess players and their games were legendary. Professor Kettering won slightly more often than Walter. Scarrabo and Antonio would watch, whispering advice. Scarrabo was always on Professor Kettering's side and Antonio helped Walter. If Walter's situation was hopeless, he would use one of his tricks to replace a piece on the board that Professor Kettering had already taken. It would take her a minute or two to realise that something odd had happened and then Walter Flood would throw up his hands and admit defeat.

One evening, Walter had set up the chess board and the game had already begun. He had made a strong start, taking three of Professor Kettering's pieces before she took even one of his, but Professor Kettering had

fought back. At this stage it wasn't possible to say who was going to win. It was Walter's move.

Antonio was concentrating very hard. He couldn't make up his mind what advice to give. First he thought Walter should do one thing, then he thought he should do another. It was an important stage of the game. Antonio tried to work out the consequences of the two moves he had in mind.

'Antonio,' said Scarrabo.

Antonio didn't look up. It was probably just a trick by Scarrabo to break his concentration.

'Antonio,' said Scarrabo, 'I think someone wants to talk to you.'

'Where?' Antonio was still gazing at the chessboard.

'There,' said Scarrabo.

Now Antonio did look up. Scarrabo nodded towards the entrance of the great house. There was Mr Guzman, walking slowly towards them, and wearing, as always, his Homburger hat.

Antonio stared. He felt as if he couldn't even move. He just stared.

The game stopped. Walter, who had just picked up a bishop to make his move, held the piece in midair. Everyone watched Mr Guzman.

Finally the great actor arrived at the deckchairs.

'Professor Kettering,' he said in a gentle voice, removing his hat and taking Professor Kettering's hand. 'Scarrabo,' he said, turning to the magician. 'And ...'

'Walter Flood,' said Scarrabo.

'Mr Flood,' said Mr Guzman, nodding correctly.

Scarrabo stood up. He put his hands on Antonio's shoulders: 'Antonio.'

'Yes,' said Mr Guzman. 'Antonio. I wonder if Antonio would do me the honour of walking a little way with me. It is a very fine evening for a walk.'

'It is a fine evening for a walk,' said Professor Kettering, who couldn't keep the hint of a schoolgirl blush out of her face.

Antonio felt Scarrabo's hands on his shoulders, nudging him forward.

CHAPTER 13

They walked towards the hedge that ran beside the lawn. Patches of the grass had gone dry and brown during the summer. Mr Guzman walked slowly, leaning some of his weight on his cane. Antonio could have gone twice as fast.

Mr Guzman had the palest blue eyes that Antonio had ever seen. He had a white moustache that was as thin as a line. He was wearing a very nice black suit with fine pinstripes and Antonio could see a gold chain that was attached to something in the pocket of his waistcoat, probably a watch. Mr Guzman's shirt had a long, old-fashioned collar and he wore a silk tie of dark red with large blue diamonds, tied perfectly in a triangular knot. His Homburger hat was dark blue. It looked very elegant, Antonio thought, glancing up at it. That was odd. It had never occurred to him before that the Homburger hat looked very elegant, he had only thought about its funny name.

Antonio remembered what Professor Kettering had said about Theodore Guzman, that he was so handsome, so dashing. If Mr Guzman's face were younger, if the thin white moustache were a line of black instead, if he had a mop of dark hair instead of the mostly bald head that was under his hat, and if his thin body had filled out the nice suit that he was wearing, Professor Kettering would be right. Mr Guzman would look very dashing indeed.

Mr Guzman didn't say anything. Antonio thought he must be concentrating on the effort of walking. He didn't often go so far. His shoes were polished so well that Antonio could see the sky reflected in them. He must be hot. It was a warm evening, too warm to be dressed up as if you were going out to meet the mayor.

Mr Guzman stopped when they came to the edge of the grass. He looked up and down the hedge. Further along there was an old stone bench. It was one of the few things that were left over from old duke's days, when the lawn was just the tiniest fraction of the vast parks that surrounded his house. Sometimes, after a hard day's work, Mr Carman sat there with his wife for half an hour, keeping an eye on the entrance to the house in case he were needed.

Mr Guzman and Antonio sat on the bench. Mr Guzman took a large white handkerchief out of his pocket and mopped his brow.

Across the lawn, Scarrabo and Professor Kettering and Walter Flood were still sitting on the deck chairs. Walter was leaning over the chess board. Professor Kettering was pouring more iced tea into her glass.

Antonio wondered what had happened after Walter moved the bishop.

Mr Guzman was watching them as well. 'Do you play chess, Antonio?' he asked.

'Yes,' said Antonio, 'but not as well as Mama.'

'Which is your favourite piece?' asked Mr Guzman.

Antonio frowned. 'Different pieces are good in different situations.'

'True. But each one has a different personality. Like people. Take the knight. Oh, he is a cunning creature. You don't even notice him there—then suddenly he jumps at you from around the corner and swallows you up.'

Mr Guzman had a very expressive voice. When he talked about the knight you felt as if you were watching a cat suddenly leap at a mouse.

'The castle is upstanding and honest. There he stands, and he can only move up and down, backwards and forwards, the stout fellow. Be warned, he says, here I am.'

'Then the queen is my favourite piece,' said Antonio.

'Why?'

'The queen can do the most things.'

'Then she is the most useful piece,' said Mr Guzman, 'she is the most powerful piece. That doesn't mean she has to be your favourite piece. We do not always like the most those who are most powerful. To me, for instance, the personality of the queen does not appeal at all. The queen is arrogant and boastful. Look at me, she says, see how powerful I am. Take care, or I will win this game all by myself!'

Walter's hand moved over the board. Professor Kettering leaned forward.

'Mr Flood has made his move,' said Mr Guzman. 'He took a long time.'

'Which is *your* favourite piece?' asked Antonio.

'The king,' said Mr Guzman without hesitation.

'But the king's the *worst* piece! He can hardly do anything at all. All the king can do is lose the game. That's all he's there for.'

'Yes, but isn't there something grand about him? He is weak, yet the whole game revolves around him. He is powerless, yet everywhere others fight for his life. Isn't there something both sad and majestic about him? To me, Antonio, the king is a puzzle. What is he? It is as if he has his mind on higher things. It is as if he is a great thinker, or a great poet, and he cannot be distracted. It is for others to protect him.'

Professor Kettering reached out over the board.

'That was a quick move,' observed Mr Guzman.

'I think Mama is going to win,' said Antonio. 'When she starts to make her moves that quickly, Walter has lost his advantage.'

They watched the game from a distance. Professor Kettering's moves became quicker and quicker.

'Your friend is very talented,' said Mr Guzman.

'Who, Walter Flood? No. Mama is a better player, but sometimes Walter manages to beat her.'

Mr Guzman smiled. 'No, Antonio. Your friend. The boy who ate all that food.'

'Oh, you mean Ralph Robinson.'

'You know, Antonio, I meant to speak to you long ago. About your play. I meant to thank you. I hope you will forgive me. I have been unwell, and it has only been in the last few days that I have been able to leave my apartment.'

'Then you've missed almost the whole summer!'

'Has it been a good summer?' asked Mr Guzman.

'Not bad. There have been a lot of cloudy days.'

'Well, that can happen. You know, Antonio, that boy has talent. The last scene where he ate all those hamburgers, that showed real ability. I was never a true comic actor myself, but when I was younger I knew some of the best in the country. Now, Antonio, a comic actor will tell you he is doing well if he can keep an audience laughing by himself for even two minutes. For that reason most of them won't do a scene that lasts longer than that. People just stop laughing. And how long did it take for Ralph to eat those hamburgers? Five minutes, or even six? And still the audience laughed. Many actors would have refused even to try it.'

'Ralph has decided to be a humorous actor,' said Antonio.

'Good,' said Mr Guzman. 'I am sure he will be a great success.'

Professor Kettering had won the chess game. You could see by the way Walter Flood threw up his hands. Maybe if Antonio had been there to help he would have had a better chance.

Scarrabo and Walter started folding up the deckchairs. Professor Kettering collected the tea glasses. Scarrabo turned towards the bench.

'Antonio, we're going in,' he called out. 'Come up when you're ready.'

Antonio nodded. Scarrabo and Walter took a deckchair in each hand and started walking back to the great house. Professor Kettering walked between them, carrying the tray with the jug and glasses.

Antonio looked at Mr Guzman. 'Did you really like our play? Truly?'

'Yes,' said Mr Guzman. 'Truly. I liked it very much. That is why I wanted to thank you.'

'But it didn't have a stage, and there weren't any costumes, and all we had were a table and a couple of chairs.'

'So?' Mr Guzman chuckled. 'Antonio, people say my greatest performance was Hamlet. And that may be right. It *was* a great performance. I wouldn't brag about it, but it's the truth. There was a wonderful set designed by a man called Patrick Munet, and the costumes were designed by Marika Bell. You would not have heard of them, but they were the finest designers of the day. And all the other actors in that play were excellent. It makes it easier to give a great performance when everything around you is just right. But if you ask me, Antonio, my greatest performance was a play called *Song of the Mermaid*. Yet it didn't have fine costumes and there weren't any sets. And it wasn't even in a theatre.'

'Where was it?'

'In a village. On a beach.'

Mr Guzman paused for a moment. Antonio watched him. Mr Guzman's pale blue eyes were staring at the great house. In the rosy sunset, the stone of its walls glowed. But Antonio had the feeling that Mr Guzman wasn't seeing the house at all.

'On a beach, with the sand between my toes,' remembered Mr Guzman. He looked at Antonio. 'Do you know *Song of the Mermaid*, Antonio? When I was your age every child knew *Song of the Mermaid*. The story comes from a very old folk tale about a sailor who is captivated by a mermaid he spotted in the sea during one of his voyages. The mermaid sings her irresistible song, asking him to join her. But he doesn't. What would happen to him in the water? Wouldn't he drown? He is too frightened to take the leap over the side of his boat. Years later, when the sailor is too old to sail and can only sit on the jetty and watch the fishing boats sail in and out of the harbour, the mermaid returns for him. He is old but she is as young as ever. Mermaids never age. Once more she beckons him. Come into the sea, she says. And this time, he has nothing to lose. Slowly he lowers himself over the side of the jetty and into the water.'

Mr Guzman smiled.

'Every language has its stories and plays about mermaids. The sea has always made men think of impossible mysteries. *Song of the Mermaid* is one of those plays. When you are a child you think it is just a fairy-tale, and when you are older you realise it is a play for adults as well. One summer I took a holiday on the coast, and it just so happened that the village nearby had a tra-dition that the events in *Song of the Mermaid* happened right there, that the story told the tale of one of their own fishermen. Of course this was nonsense, Antonio. For a start there are no mermaids, and anyway you will find that every fishing village in the world thinks it is the place where one of these fairy tales happened. Still, in this village, every summer, the young people put on a performance of the play on the beach. This performance was always held at night, during the first full moon after midsummer. Don't ask me why, it was just a tradition.

'Anyway, when the fishermen heard I was staying at the house outside their village, they came to me and asked whether I would do them the honour of taking the main role in the play. At first I said no. I did not want to take the part out of the hands of the local youth who was meant to play it. But they begged and begged. The one who was meant to play the part begged loudest of all. Maybe he just didn't want to perform. In the end I said yes. I knew the part. In fact, I had performed it in the city only the year before. Once I learn a part, Antonio, I remember it forever.'

Forever, thought Antonio. Every line? Forever?

'Could you still remember it now?'

'I could,' replied Mr Guzman. 'To remember a part you have only to remember who is the character you are playing, to understand what he is like. The words follow from that.'

'And you played the part, in the village?'

'Yes, Antonio. That very night. The sun went down, the stars came out, and the whole village marched down to the beach. No one would miss it. Old people who were too frail to walk were carried onto the sand. What costumes did we have? Only the rags of fishermen, which real fishermen had been wearing the day before. What was our stage? Only the sand of the beach, the coarse grass of the dunes, the mouth of a cave and the foot of a cliff. What spotlights did we have? Only the light of the full moon and the flicker of torches. Who were our actors? Only the young men and women of the village. But Antonio, that night, we acted as if we were the children of the stars, as if the heavens themselves were watching us, as if the beams of the full moon painted us with the colours of gods, gave us voices of honey, gave us spirits divine.'

Mr Guzman's eyes were closed. He did not even breathe.

Antonio said: 'Mr Guzman, are you too old for acting now?'

Mr Guzman opened his eyes. A very brief smile came across his lips. There was more pain than happiness in that smile.

'There is no age that is too old for acting, Antonio. I am not well enough. But not too old.'

Suddenly Antonio felt very sad. He turned away to hide his face. He felt as if he might suddenly start crying. It was ridiculous.

'Antonio, what has happened to the Dolphin Theatre?'

Antonio shrugged.

'*I* have a theatre, Antonio. Would you like to see it?'

CHAPTER 14

Antonio knew something about theatres. For instance, he had sometimes been in Scarrabo's dressing room after a performance. A dressing room always has a table with a mirror and a chair in front of it. It can have armchairs as well, and a washbasin, and a low table where people can put their glasses if you have a bottle of champagne to celebrate the show. Antonio had also seen Walter Flood and Louisa Roberts arranging the equipment for Scarrabo's performance on stage. The lighting man was somewhere high up in the dark theatre, and when Walter called out to him to test the spotlights they went on and off like sharp fingers of light jabbing you in the face. He had seen how the curtains are operated, and how you can stand at the side of the stage during a performance and see everything without the audience even knowing that you are there. Antonio had seen enough to know that the part of a theatre that is behind the curtain is bigger and much more interesting than the part that is in front of it.

When Scarrabo asked Antonio what he had talked about with Mr Guzman, he said that Mr Guzman had talked about acting, and he told him about Mr Guzman's performance in *Song of the Mermaid*. When Professor Kettering asked him what they talked about, he said Mr Guzman talked about chess, and he told her that Mr Guzman's favourite piece was the king. And all of this was true. Mr Guzman *had* talked about acting and about chess. But Antonio did not tell anyone that Mr Guzman said he had a theatre. That, Antonio felt, was something that Mr Guzman had meant for him alone.

Antonio expected that Mr Guzman owned some theatre in the city. He was probably going to take him around behind the stage, and show him where they kept the props and the sets from old productions, and maybe let him sit in on a rehearsal. Since he knew about theatres, this did not excite him as much as it might have excited another boy. But he did want to hear the stories that Mr Guzman would tell in his deep expressive voice, like the story about the village by the sea and *Song of the Mermaid*. There must be lots of other things that he could tell about the plays he had performed and all the places he had been. An actor as dashing as Mr Guzman, Antonio thought, must have as many amazing stories to tell about his life as Scarrabo could tell about the Duke's House.

Three days later, at three o'clock in the afternoon, precisely as Mr Guzman had told him, Antonio knocked on the blue door with the big gold handle. It took a few minutes for Mr Guzman to answer, but this time Antonio knocked only once and waited. Mr Guzman was dressed the same as always, in a dark suit with a perfectly knotted tie, except he wasn't wearing his Homburger hat. He asked Antonio to come in.

In the entrance hall of Mr Guzman's apartment was a small chandelier made of pieces of crystal. The light that flashed from it was the colour of roses and honey. At the opposite end of the hall hung a splendid oil painting of a man standing in a wood in the autumn. The man was dressed in very old fashioned clothes with a strange three-cornered hat. The frame around the painting was richly carved and painted in gold.

On each side of the hallway were three closed doors. Mr Guzman lead Antonio into the second room on the left, where there was a long white sofa with two matching armchairs. The room had a white marble fireplace, and above it hung another painting, showing a golden, cone-shaped haystack in a field. Antonio sat down and sank deep into the soft cushions of one of the armchairs. The cushions had thick gold tassels at the corners. Then Mr Guzman asked Antonio if he wanted a drink. Antonio wasn't really very thirsty.

'I have some lemonade,' said Mr Guzman. 'I'm sure that you will like it.'

Mr Guzman went out. Antonio turned his head and

looked around the room, searching for the poster that he had glimpsed from the secret passage. It wasn't there. The other walls had pictures of wildflowers. They were much smaller and much more watery than the painting of the haystack that hung over the fireplace.

Mr Guzman's apartment looked as if someone had carefully arranged the furniture and then nothing was ever moved or touched. It was as if you came through the door into a place where everything was very still and slow, like Mr Guzman himself. There was nothing at all lying around on the floor.

Mr Guzman came back with a tray, which he put on a low table that was in front of the fireplace.

'I learned how to make this from a lady who worked

at the old Apollo Theatre,'
he said, pouring two glasses
of lemonade. 'It's lime. She
would make me a jug every evening.

I would drink half of it between the first two acts, and
half between the last two acts. It's very hot on stage,
Antonio. This lime lemonade kept me going. I begged
her to give me the recipe. In the end she did, on the con-
dition that I never reveal it to anyone else. The secret is
that the limes must be perfectly fresh. I can say no more.'

Antonio sipped the lime-flavoured lemonade. It had a
tangy taste and wasn't sweet at all. Somewhere at the
back of it you could taste the skin of the lime.

'What do you think?' Mr Guzman asked.

Antonio frowned. 'I'm not sure,' he said.

Mr Guzman laughed. 'You must be careful with this
lemonade, Antonio. The more you drink of it, the more
you will like it.'

Mr Guzman drank his lemonade. He seemed to be
staring at the paintings of wildflowers behind Antonio's
head.

When they finished the lemonade Mr Guzman stood
up. 'Come, Antonio.'

Antonio followed Mr Guzman into a room on the
other side of the corridor. He thought Mr Guzman must
be going to fetch his Homburger hat before they went
out to his theatre.

This room was not like the other one. Its walls were made of wood panelling. Mr Guzman went to a cupboard in the corner. There, on the wall right beside him, was the poster! Antonio recognised it at once: the gold letters and the red background. But this time he could see it in full.

THEODORE
GUZMAN
stars in
HAMLET
at the
APOLLO THEATRE

Antonio turned and looked for the crack in the opposite wall. The wood panels were very old and there were tiny gaps between some of them. There must have been a crack in the bricks behind one of those gaps. Antonio couldn't help feeling guilty at the memory of secretly peeping into the room where he was standing now.

Mr Guzman glanced around and saw Antonio staring at the other wall.

'It's foolish, isn't it?' he said.

Antonio didn't know what he meant. Having cracks in your walls wasn't foolish, it was just bad luck.

'All these posters.'

Antonio looked around the room properly. Now he understood what Mr Guzman was talking about. There were at least three posters on every wall, each one of them carefully framed in gold. 'Theodore Guzman stars in *this*', 'Theodore Guzman stars in *that*', 'Theodore Guzman stars at *this* theatre', 'Theodore Guzman stars at *that* theatre'.

'It's foolish, I know,' repeated Mr Guzman. 'I've put these posters up. I have many more, of course, but I never take them out. *These* plays all meant something to me.'

Mr Guzman closed the cupboard, holding a small key in his hand. Just beneath the *Hamlet* poster was a tiny lock. There was a door in the wood panelling.

'The wonderful thing about this old house, Antonio,' said Mr Guzman as he fiddled with the lock, 'is that it has different rooms. All sorts of rooms, odd rooms that you would never even imagine were there, rooms you would never find in a new house. Because it wasn't built like a new house. When this house was built, it was meant to have everything. It was meant to be like a small world in itself.'

Mr Guzman opened the door. The Hamlet poster swung back. It was not a big door and Mr Guzman stooped as he went through. It seemed like a lot of trouble, thought Antonio, to have to go through so many doors and locks just to get a hat, even if it was an elegant blue Homburger.

After a few seconds Mr Guzman's head reappeared. 'Antonio, what are you waiting for?'

Antonio was puzzled. 'Aren't we going out to visit your theatre?'

Mr Guzman laughed. He gestured to the open door. '*This* is my theatre.'

CHAPTER 15

Mr Guzman's theatre was a single room.

The room had eight equal sides, just as if a mathematician had designed it, and not a single window. The eight walls rose vertically and then sloped inwards in long, tapering triangles to meet at a point high above the floor. A lantern hung from the centre on a long chain.

Mr Guzman was right. Who would have imagined that there was such a room within the Duke's House?

'What was it used for?' asked Antonio.

'This room? They say the old duke was fond of alchemy, Antonio. Maybe his alchemists did their experiments here. Trying to make gold out of blocks of chalk.'

Antonio laughed.

'Oh, yes,' said Mr Guzman. 'Gold out of chalk. That's what the alchemists tried to do. With all sorts of spells and mathematical formulas. It was not allowed, of course, and a person would face terrible punishment if he were discovered. Now, look at this room, Antonio. Can't you imagine an alchemist in here, secretly working with his instruments and books? I can. Look at the

shape of this room, the angles, the lengths, the proportions. Only if everything were mathematically perfect,
even the room in which he worked, could the alchemist
succeed, and only if he were completely undisturbed by
the outside world.'

Mr Guzman closed the door through which they had
entered. Now the room was a flawless whole. Each wall
mirrored exactly the one opposite it, like a cut jewel.
And they were inside it.

'This room is perfect. And perfectly secret. But
luckily for us, there are no longer any alchemists who
want to use it! So, let us sit, Antonio.'

There were two benches placed beside each other
about half way across the room. They were covered in
dark leather and their wooden legs curved gracefully
to the floor, ending in feet the shape of lion paws.
Against six of the eight walls in the room stood tall
cabinets made of plain, uncarved wood, and in front of
the seventh wall, directly opposite the door, stood a
miniature stage.

'You see,' said Mr Guzman, when they were each sitting on one of the benches facing the stage, 'now we are
the audience.'

The stage was built of wood and its full height was as
tall as Mr Guzman. The platform of the stage itself was
about halfway up, and it was framed by a triangular
top and columns at the side. Below the platform was a

wooden panel with a carved rose in the middle. The rose had rings and rings of tiny petals. There was also a carving on the triangle at the very top of the stage, a great horn that looked like a seashell, containing fruits and nuts and flowers that spilled out of it, across the top and down the columns on either side. It looked as if every fruit and flower in the world were there; wherever your eyes happened to rest you saw something different.

Antonio went over to the stage. He examined the carving on one of the columns. It looked so real, as if a cascade of fruits and nuts had suddenly been frozen and transformed, by some sort of magic, into wood.

He touched the wood. It was smooth and had a rich, yellowy hue. There were dark veins running through it. The panel below the stage reflected the yellow light from the lantern.

'My father was a carver,' said Mr Guzman from behind Antonio. 'Mostly he was a stone carver. Actually, he mostly carved tombstones.'

Antonio heard Mr Guzman laugh as he recollected.

'He could carve anything, my father. Some of the little toys he made for me when I was a boy! Five minutes with a piece of wood and you would have something. A horse, a pigeon, anything. He loved to carve wood. Any kind of wood. Unfortunately, people did not want many things carved of wood. They wanted tombstones. So that's what he carved, nine times out of ten.'

'Did he carve this?' asked Antonio, running his finger over the knobbles of a carved bunch of grapes.

'This? No. If my father had carved this, you would know it. Then it really would be something, instead of the poor attempt that it is.'

Antonio did not think it was a poor attempt. If Antonio had carved something like this, it was not likely that he would hide it in a room with no windows.

'Did you carve it?'

'Yes. Do you want to hear a strange thing? Originally I was going to be a carver too, like my father. I had done almost three years of my apprenticeship. My father sent me to another master carver. A father cannot teach a son, he said. But then I became an actor. I suppose I had always been a performer. When the master carver was out of the studio I used to impersonate him. He had a way of swinging his hammer and swearing and spitting out of the corner of his mouth. Sometimes he swore and spat at the same time, which is not as easy as it sounds. It took me months to teach myself how to do it. When he was out of the studio no one did any work. All the other apprentices were too busy rolling on the floor with laughter at my impersonation. I also gave performances of the dramatic fights he had with his wife. My carving did not improve very much, but my acting did. In the end I had to admit I was better at acting than carving.'

Mr Guzman chuckled.

'By the way,' he added, 'in case you want to know, it's walnut wood. Forget mahogany, rosewood, teak. Remember, Antonio, if you want to carve something, carve in walnut. The prince of woods. Hard to find a piece that's good enough to carve from, but it's worth looking for. Don't you agree?'

Antonio nodded. He was still examining the stage. It was empty. Deep at the back of it there was only a bare wooden board.

'Mr Guzman, if we are the audience, what are we meant to watch?'

'I was wondering when you were going to ask me that,' said Mr Guzman, smiling. He stood up and went to the nearest cabinet. 'Here, Antonio. The theatre is in here.'

Antonio looked at him blankly.

'In some ways this is a theatre, Antonio, and in some ways this is a history of the theatre. And in another way, this is new theatre. As much new theatre as your mind can imagine. Do you understand?'

'No.'

Mr Guzman laughed. It was the merriest laugh that Antonio had heard from him, happy, amused and light-hearted. Antonio laughed as well. He didn't know what he was laughing at, but he couldn't help it.

'I wouldn't understand either, if someone explained it like that,' admitted Mr Guzman. 'Look, Antonio,' he said, and he opened the lower door of the cabinet.

There was a flash of colour. The inside of the door was covered in gleaming daubs of paint, and the cavity of the cabinet was bright.

Antonio stared. It was unexpected. The room was so stark, with its wooden floor and wooden cabinets and carved stage and bare white walls. And then, suddenly, this cabinet was full of colour, as if the solemn room had been hiding a lively heart all along.

'All of these cabinets ... ?' Antonio asked after a moment.

'Yes,' said Mr Guzman.

The inside of the cabinet door had a series of ledges, and in the slots along each ledge were carved figures painted in all colours and styles. The colours were vivid, fresh, as if the paint had just dried. Inside the cabinet stood a set of flat wooden boards. The one that was visible at the front was also painted in bold and striking colours.

The board showed the interior of a great palace lit by flaming torches. There were columns of marble and rich scarlet curtains, and in the background a long banqueting table was covered with the remains of a lavish meal. A dog was gnawing at a bone at the foot of one of the columns.

'Do you recognise it?' asked Mr Guzman.

Antonio shook his head.

'The background for the first scene of *The Sicilian Cavalier*, exactly as it was at the Tower Theatre twenty years ago. When I played Don Marco in *The Sicilian Cavalier* we had a real table like that at the back of the stage. Every afternoon one of the stagehands went round all the nearby restaurants collecting lunch scraps to throw across the table for the evening performance.'

Mr Guzman took the board out of the cabinet and carried it to the stage. He opened a side panel and slid the board into a groove at the back. Suddenly, the stage no longer looked empty.

Mr Guzman reached around and flicked a switch. A light went on inside the top of the stage. Suddenly, it was bright.

Antonio sat down on one of the benches again. Now he knew what Mr Guzman meant. It really was like being in a theatre. It was like looking into a palace after a banquet had taken place.

Mr Guzman had already gone back to the open cabinet and selected three figures from the slots in the door. He placed them on the stage: two in the middle, at the front, close to one another, as if talking; the other in the background, in a corner, beside the banquet table, as if listening.

Mr Guzman turned to face Antonio.

'Don Marco, Prince of Naples,' he said in his rich, compelling voice, gesturing gracefully at one of the figures at the front of the stage, who was wearing a cape of deep blue over his dark tunic and a silver dagger strapped to his belt. 'He is the rightful prince of Sicily. Next to him is his friend, Don Federico. A Sicilian nobleman. He is engaged to be married to Don Marco's sister, Francesca. In return for Francesca's hand he is pledged to help Don Marco overcome Don Vitello, the unlawful ruler of Sicily.'

Mr Guzman gestured to the third figure on the stage, dressed in rags.

'In the corner: a servant. Intelligent, sly, quick-witted, loyal to Don Vitello. Rafaello is his name. It is Rafaello's dream to have his own inn in the country, to have his own servants to beat and kick. Don Vitello has promised Rafaello to give him an inn if he will find a way to bring Don Marco's life to an end.'

Mr Guzman came and stood beside Antonio. His eyes were on the stage.

'The first scene. We are in the palace of Don Vitello, who has invited Don Marco to Sicily. Don Marco has accepted. Each hopes to use the occasion treacherously to do away with the other. The welcoming banquet is over. Don Marco and Don Federico are alone. In the background, out of sight, lurks the servant, Rafaello. Watch! The curtain rises ...'

CHAPTER 16

'What news, Federico?'

Don Federico glances nervously around before he speaks.
'Don Vitello rides out tonight.'

Don Marco is eager. He leaps at the news. 'Does he ride
alone?'

Don Federico laughs. A bitter laugh. Many men have

tried to catch Don Vitello alone. Few have lived to tell of their failure.

'He never rides alone. You will as soon catch the wind as you will catch Don Vitello by himself.'

'Then we must catch him in company!' exclaims Don Marco, laughing at Federico's despair. He pokes Don Federico playfully in the ribs.

Don Federico throws up his hands. 'What army do you have, Marco?'

'Where does he ride?'

'First, where is your army?'

'No, Federico. First—where does he ride?'

Don Federico rests a hand on Don Marco's shoulder. 'I love you too much to tell you where he rides, Marco.'

'Tell me where,' Don Marco demands, loudly, almost shouting, shrugging Don Federico's hand roughly away. Then once more . . . but softer this time, gently: 'Tell me where, Federico. By this will you prove your love for me.'

Don Federico sighs. He walks a few paces away and rests his head against a column. How can he hold Don Marco back? He is not strong enough to resist him. He returns to Don Marco. He whispers in his ear. He tells him the place. Three words. No more.

Don Marco clutches Federico's hand warmly. 'Then there we shall meet at midnight!'

Don Federico nods his head reluctantly. 'Yes, at midnight, Marco.'

'You, Federico, you will not fail me.'

'No, I will not fail you, Marco.'

Don Marco remains a moment longer, looking at Federico. His body is tense with energy, anticipation, fervour. His hands are clenched by his side. 'Until midnight,' he says, turns with a sweep of his cape, and leaves.

'Until midnight,' murmurs Don Federico softly. He walks slowly out from the other side of the hall.

A moment passes. Silence. Shadows.

From the background emerges the servant Rafaello. Unshaven, ragged. He glances slyly from side to side, rubs his hands.

'There is news here, there is news!' he says. His voice is hoarse, a loud, rough whisper. He laughs with cruel enjoyment. 'Much pleasure will this bring to Don Vitello— but more pleasure, and an inn, to Rafaello!'

The servant looks from side to side once more. Then he laughs again, and disappears back into the shadows . . .

Mr Guzman's voice had stopped.

Antonio looked around, as if he had been awoken from a dream. The three figures on the stage were exactly where Mr Guzman had originally placed them. But only a moment before, Antonio could have sworn, they had been moving. Don Marco in his deep blue cape had swept off the stage from the left, Don Federico in his brown cape had walked despondently off at the right,

145

and the ragged Raffaelo had come forward, gloated in a gruff whisper, and then withdrawn into the shadows.

'You do not know this play, Antonio?' asked Mr Guzman.

Antonio shook his head.

'Everyone should know this play.'

Mr Guzman got up and put the figures of Don Marco and Don Federico out of sight behind the background board. He went to the cabinet and brought another figure over to the stage. This figure was dressed in rich black clothes with a heavy gold chain around his neck, and he wore a flat black hat. The expression on his face was scowling.

'Don Vitello.'

Mr Guzman placed Rafaello next to Don Vitello. He stepped back from the stage, and began the second scene of the play.

For the next two hours Mr Guzman told *The Sicilian Cavalier*, and the voices of its characters filled the alchemy room. It was a gripping story of intrigue, treachery, cunning and suspense. By the end Don Vitello had imprisoned Francesca, Francesca had escaped with Don Federico, Don Federico had kidnapped Rafaello, Rafaello had joined Don Marco and Don Marco had triumphed over Don Vitello. Four different background boards had been used, there were twelve figures scattered around the stage, and Mr Guzman had collapsed on one of the benches, exhausted, hoarse, just like an actor who has finished an epic performance.

'That is the first time I have performed *The Sicilian Cavalier* in twenty years,' said Mr Guzman, his eyes closed.

Antonio was still thinking about the play: the violent Don Vitello, the calculating Rafaello, the impetuous Don Marco, the determined Francesca, the gentle Don Federico. Poor Don Federico, he seemed out of place amidst so much treachery and ruthlessness. He had barely managed to kidnap Rafaello, even though Rafaello had already decided to betray his master and actually wanted to be taken.

Eventually Antonio said: 'Shall I put the pieces away?'

'I would be very grateful,' said Mr Guzman, whose eyes were still closed.

Antonio put the figures back in the slots in the cabinet door. He pulled the boards out of the stage and carried them across the room.

'Shall I switch off the light?' he asked after he had put everything away and closed the door of the cabinet.

'Yes please,' said Mr Guzman.

Antonio found the switch for the stage light. He turned it off and went back to his seat. The stage was empty and dark once more. The room was just as it was before Mr Guzman had opened the cabinet door. Bare and stark.

Compared to the story of Don Marco and Don Federico, rich with plots and conspiracies, *Four Stories* seemed like a baby's tale. Antonio wondered what other plays were inside all those other cabinets.

'Plays I have done,' said Mr Guzman.

'All the plays in the world,' said Antonio, as much to himself as to Mr Guzman.

'No, only plays I have done, Antonio. And not even every one of them. The ones that were important, the ones that meant something. That's why I say my theatre is a history of the past. In some ways, it is a history of all the best plays.'

'But only when you tell them, like you told *The Sicilian Cavalier*.'

'No,' replied Mr Guzman, 'that's not quite right. Even when I do not tell them, my theatre is a history. The scenes, the costumes of the figures, they are the scenes and the costumes of designers who by now are old or even dead. The costume of Don Vitello—that is the costume that Sidney Monk wore when he played opposite me at the Tower Theatre. You cannot find those things anywhere else. The designs are gone and people have forgotten them. Only in my theatre do they exist.'

Mr Guzman smiled wistfully.

'When I tell the plays, Antonio, that is something different. That's why I said this is also a theatre of the present, like any other theatre. If you know the plays, as

I know them, they can be performed here. But there is something more about this theatre, Antonio. It is not only a theatre of the past, and of the present, but of the future as well.'

Mr Guzman was looking very intensely at Antonio, as one looks at someone when trying to see if he understands. And Antonio was gazing at the empty stage, as one gazes emptily at something when concentrating very hard on what one is hearing.

'Consider, Antonio. In that cabinet are the characters from *The Sicilian Cavalier*, and on the shelf above them are the characters from *A Company of Sleepwalkers*. In another cabinet is *Hamlet* and somewhere else is Marian from *The Rose of Carlisle*. Here, in this room, hundreds of characters sleep side by side, waiting to be awoken. But in the normal theatre they never meet. You perform *Hamlet* one year, and next year you perform *A Company of Sleepwalkers*, and maybe someone else in another theatre is performing *The Rose of Carlisle* or maybe you yourself perform it another time in another place. They are all separate. But here, Antonio, in this theatre, there are no limitations. There is no need for them to be separate. Forget the past. Here, the future is limited only by your imagination.'

Mr Guzman stood up. Suddenly he had new energy. He went back to the cabinet and pulled Don Federico off the door. Then he went across the room to another cabinet and extracted a figure in a green doublet with a floppy green hat hanging down over his ear.

'Hamlet,' he announced, setting the new figure down on the stage. 'Don Federico,' he said, slapping the familiar figure down beside him. 'Don't worry about the scenery.'

Antonio ran across and switched on the stage light.

'Look, Antonio,' said Mr Guzman, bringing him back to the bench. 'Hamlet and Don Federico. But stop! You are seeing something new. It has never happened before. Hamlet and Don Federico? Side by side? You are at the limit of imagination. Until this moment, Antonio, Don Federico has always been trapped in *The Sicilian Cavalier* and Hamlet has always been locked in his own play. But now they are both free. What would they say to one another? Think. They are both gentle men. Yet Don Federico, as gentle as he is, finds himself plotting to bring down Don Vitello. Now, Hamlet, for your information, is the son of a king, who was brought down by his own brother, Hamlet's uncle. Already we have found something new just by putting Don Federico and Hamlet side by side. Does Don Vitello have a son who, like Hamlet, will see his father fall? Have we ever thought about him before? Has Don Federico ever thought about him? If we leave Don Federico and Hamlet together for a few minutes to talk quietly, what will happen to Don Federico? Will he still be so eager to

150

bring down Don Vitello? What would he say?'

Antonio frowned. The two figures, green and brown, Hamlet and Don Federico, stood face to face, as if whispering.

'What *would* he say?' said Antonio, waiting for Mr Guzman to perform Don Federico's speech.

'I don't know,' said Mr Guzman. He laughed. 'He has never said it before. You must think, Antonio.'

Antonio thought. 'He would say . . .'

'What, Antonio? Say it.'

Antonio frowned. 'He would say . . . "Do we really need to bring Don Vitello down?"'

'To whom? To Hamlet?'

'No, to Don Marco.'

'Then get Don Marco, Antonio.'

Antonio ran and grabbed the impetuous Don Marco from his niche and put him on the stage near Don Federico.

'But we should leave Hamlet on the stage, Antonio, in the background, so we can feel his presence.'

Antonio moved Hamlet back.

'Now, Antonio.'

Antonio said: 'Marco, do we really need to bring Don Vitello down?'

Mr Guzman replied with Don Marco's scornful laughter: 'What is this, Federico?'

Antonio considered his next line. Mr Guzman watched him closely.

'What is this Federico,' Mr Guzman repeated, 'have you lost your courage?'

'No, Marco,' said Antonio after a moment, 'it isn't my courage.'

'What then? Do you doubt me, will you betray me?'

'Why do you need to be the king of Sicily as well? You are already the prince in Naples.'

'You *will* betray me! What has Don Vitello said to you, what has he promised you?'

'No, Marco,' Antonio cried. 'Think about his son.'

'The son of Don Vitello? What is the son of Don Vitello to me?'

Antonio did not answer. Instead, he went to the stage and drew Hamlet from the shadows, placing him between Don Federico and Don Marco.

'Who is this?' demanded Mr Guzman. 'By his clothes, I say he is a foreigner.'

'I am.'

'Then what are you to me?'

'I am the son of a king,' said Antonio,

'Then when I am king of Sicily I will greet you as a king,' replied Mr Guzman.

'How are you going to become king of Sicily?'

'I will bring down the tyrant who rules in my place.'

'A man said he would do that to my father.'

'And did he?' asked Mr Guzman in a quieter tone.

'Yes,' said Antonio sadly. 'It was my uncle.'

Mr Guzman looked at Antonio. 'What will Don Marco do now, Antonio?'

Antonio thought. 'I think he will ignore Hamlet, after a little while.'

'Yes,' said Mr Guzman. 'I think you are right. That is Don Marco's character. But what about Don Federico? Do you think he will ignore Hamlet?'

'No. Don Federico could not ignore Hamlet.'

'So what will happen to Don Marco?'

'He will go ahead without Don Federico's help.'

'Perhaps he will turn on Don Federico as well, and throw him into chains.'

Antonio considered. 'He might.'

Mr Guzman smiled. 'You have to work it out, Antonio. There is no limit here but the limit of your own imagination.'

Antonio put the figures away in their niches. Don Marco, Don Federico and Hamlet. Mr Guzman was starting to look tired again.

'I hardly ever go to the theatre,' said Antonio.

'You must make sure to change that. But the best plays are not always in the theatre, Antonio. Or I should say, any place where you perform a play is a theatre.'

'Like the beach near a fishing village,' said Antonio.

'Yes, why not? Or the lawn in front of a house.'

Mr Guzman turned to Antonio. Suddenly the gaze from his pale blue eyes was penetrating, searching, as if there were an important matter that he was trying to decide.

After a moment he said: 'The trouble, Antonio, is that I am old now, and not very well, and yet there is no one else who knows how to use the theatre. No one else has even seen it.'

'*No one?*'

'Some have probably guessed that it exists. One or two of my friends, who were certain, even asked to view it. But no one else has been in this room, until you, Antonio.' Mr Guzman paused. 'I am still not sure if I was right to bring you here.'

Antonio did not understand.

'Antonio, there is room in the theatre for one more play. It must be a special one. Until I saw your play on the lawn outside, I did not think that I would ever find it.'

Antonio gasped. 'You don't mean *Four Stories?* Mr Guzman, that was just a children's play. It didn't have a stage, or a script, or a . . .'

Mr Guzman put his finger to his lips, silencing him. 'Antonio, I cannot perform *Four Stories*. I do not know it.'

Antonio stared at Mr Guzman.

'You will have to perform it, Antonio.'

'But Mr Guzman, it's just a children's—'

'So, Antonio? Does it matter how old you are when you create a play?'

'Well, I barely even acted in it. I just organised it, Mr Guzman. It was the others. It was *their* stories.'

'Antonio, wasn't it your story as well?'

Antonio did not reply. Mr Guzman was looking at him with a deep, knowing gaze. There was nowhere to hide from it.

Eventually Mr Guzman said: 'There is a key to the theatre, and it tells which plays are in it and where every character is. Once a person has this key, Antonio, all three parts of the theatre are his: the past, the present and the future. But he cannot have the key if he has never performed in the theatre. How would he know how to use it?'

Antonio looked up at Mr Guzman.

'Now you must decide, Antonio, what you will do. There was a reason that you decided to stage a play on the lawn outside, wasn't there?'

Yes, there was a reason. But it wasn't so that he would have to perform all by himself in front of the great actor, who could remember every word of every part that he had ever played. It wasn't to perform a play that five children had made up, in a room where the characters of all the greatest plays in the world would watch him. And it wasn't to get the key to a theatre that contained the past and the present and the future in one place. Back then, he hadn't even known about the alchemy room and the secret theatre within it. The reason had never been as complicated or as difficult as this.

'Sometimes life is like a play, Antonio. Often, when you start a play, you think you know how it is going to end, but then it does not turn out as you expect. In life, sometimes you start something, and you think you are in control of it and you know exactly which direction it is going, and then suddenly you find it has a will of its own and is taking you somewhere else. Perhaps somewhere interesting and exciting, and perhaps a bit frightening as well. And then you must decide, when this happens: are you going to take a chance and continue, or are you going to jump off and turn back? It may be daunting to take the chance, and it may be easier to refuse it. But the person who never takes the chance, never changes, and everything he sees is the same from one day to the next.' Mr Guzman paused, still watching him. 'So now, Antonio, you must decide.'

Antonio did not reply.

'Don't rush,' said Mr Guzman. 'Don't imagine that it will be easy. This theatre is unlike any other. To perform in this theatre, one must take the part of every character. One must become not merely one actor, but many. The whole play must be inside your head, you must feel it, know it, believe in it, and you alone must bring it out, every word, every movement. You alone.'

Antonio frowned. 'Will you help me?'

'I will help you, but it is you who must decide. Think well. That is how I will discover whether I was right. You see, Antonio, I have already taken *my* chance, by bringing you to my theatre.'

'You were right, Mr Guzman.'

'No, first you must decide. Then you must show me.'

Mr Guzman gazed at Antonio. Antonio thought for a moment longer. Then he nodded.

Mr Guzman smiled. It was the kind of smile that one shares with another person who is facing a difficult task. 'Good. I am very glad. Now, there are many things I must prepare before you can perform the play. I will let you know when it is time to come back.'

'How?'

'Patience, Antonio. You will see.' He sighed. 'I am rather tired now. I will sit here for a little while. Can you find your way out?'

'Yes.'

'Then I will let you know when I am ready. Don't worry. I will give you some warning first.'

Antonio got up. 'Goodbye, Mr Guzman.'

'Goodbye, Antonio.'

Antonio left the theatre. Outside, he stopped for a moment and looked at the Hamlet poster again. Then he quietly left Mr Guzman's apartment, closing the front door behind him.

CHAPTER 17

The memory of Mr Guzman's theatre did not fade. The secret, perfect room, hidden deep within the Duke's House, remained as fresh in Antonio's mind as the colour of the figures that had been placed upon its stage, and the magical expressiveness of Mr Guzman's voice remained clear in his mind. He could hear each word of Hamlet's conversation with Don Marco, which had never happened anywhere before, and the sense of limitless imagination continued to tingle. Antonio was impatient to return. Yet he was also apprehensive, knowing that next time he would not be able merely to listen to Mr Guzman, but it would be he who must perform. It would not be easy, and Antonio could not tell exactly how difficult it might be. So while he yearned for Mr Guzman to call him back to the theatre, there was also a part of him that dreaded the summons to return.

It was a very strange thing, that you could both want and fear something at the same time. It had never happened to Antonio before. And there was another strange thing about it: this mixture of opposite feelings made it even harder for him to think of anything other than the moment when he would go back to Mr Guzman's theatre.

But he had to wait. The days went by and he did not hear from Mr Guzman. He knew that Mr Guzman did things slowly. It was months after *Four Stories* when he first spoke to him. But in the meantime, how was he supposed to prepare for the performance in the theatre? Maybe Simon Greene had been right, and he should have written *Four Stories* down when it was still fresh in his mind. He tried to remember the lines that the actors had said, but he knew there was a lot that he had already forgotten. And Mr Guzman's slowness didn't help. The longer Mr Guzman delayed, the more he would forget!

Patience, Antonio, he tried to tell himself. But it is easier to tell yourself about patience than to have it.

On the other hand, there was nothing patient about Ralph Robinson. He had also found a theatre to go to, and he hardly talked about anything else. Antonio got so fed up with him that he was almost tempted to tell Ralph about Mr Guzman's theatre, just to give him something different to think about. But he didn't.

Watching movies of humorous actors wasn't good enough training to be a comedian, and it hadn't taken Ralph very long to realise it. He needed to see the actors in person to learn their skills properly. And there was only one place to do that, the Variety Theatre, where they had comedy shows four times a week.

At first Ralph simply went up to the ticket-seller at the Variety Theatre and told her that he was learning to be a humorous actor and he had to be allowed in to see every show. He couldn't pay, of course. The ticket-seller didn't think Ralph needed any lessons in comedy. She told him that was one of the funniest jokes she had heard in all her years at the Variety, laughed a lot, and kicked him out.

Ralph wasn't discouraged. He would learn more by seeing the comedians backstage, anyway. So next he tried to get a job at the theatre selling ice-creams, but the manager said he was too young. Ralph had told the manager that he was four years older than he really was, and he was still too young! That was very unfair. After all, Ralph said to Antonio, people who buy ice-cream don't care about the age of the people who sell it to them. They'll buy ice-cream from a baby as long as it tastes good. And as for the people who sold the ice-creams at the Variety Theatre, most of them didn't care what sort of show went on there, they could have been selling ice-creams at the zoo for all it mattered to them. But for him, only the Variety Theatre would do. It was unfair, he kept telling Antonio, getting angrier and angrier. It was so unfair! He got so angry that one day he decided he didn't care what the manager said and he just walked up to the stage entrance an hour before the show and told the man on the door that he was there to sell ice-creams.

That was how Ralph Robinson discovered something very odd. The man on the door at the stage entrance didn't know who was really selling ice-creams and who wasn't.

'And not only that,' Ralph added, 'he believes you if you say you are!'

'But what happens once you get inside?'

'That's the best part, Antonio. No one knows what *anyone* is doing! I've never sold an ice-cream once when I've been there. When the show's on there are so many people rushing around that no one has time to notice one extra person. Yesterday the *manager* said hello to me and asked whether everything was all right. Everything was all right, but I didn't have a chance to tell him, because he had already disappeared into the lighting department.'

Within a fortnight Ralph Robinson was breezing through the stage entrance of the Variety Theatre as if he had been working there for years. He spent the summer holiday watching afternoon performances four times a week from the wings. Sometimes he stayed on for the evening show as well. Everyone in the theatre seemed to assume Ralph was working with somebody else. Ralph didn't see why they shouldn't go on believing that. He became a great favourite with the lady who darned the costumes, who fed him biscuits as she worked. She said Ralph reminded her of one of her sons when he was younger, but she couldn't quite work out why.

'Did he eat a lot?' asked Ralph.

'Now that you mention it, he did,' she said, handing Ralph another biscuit. The lady who darned the costumes thought Ralph was working with the man who repaired the stage scenery. Maybe Ralph himself had told her that. He couldn't remember.

Ralph saw all the comics rehearsing. The day Max Burroows spoke to him, Ralph almost exploded with

excitement. The great comedian only asked him for a glass of water, but when Ralph got home he rushed straight up to Antonio's apartment and made Scarrabo get him out of the bath so he could tell him.

After that, whenever Antonio saw him, Ralph was always bursting to talk about the latest comedian he had seen. It was no use trying to talk to him about *Four Stories*, to ask him to repeat the lines that he had said in one or other of the scenes. Ralph brushed the play aside with a wave of his hand, saying that he would be *ten* times funnier if he acted in it now. That was no help to Antonio, who would have to be not only as funny as Ralph, but as sad as Shoshi, as angry as Paul, and as loud as Willi, when he performed the play in Mr Guzman's theatre. But each day, as Antonio wondered whether *this* was the day when Mr Guzman was going to call him back to the alchemy room, there was nothing that Ralph wanted to do but talk about the new jokes that he had heard.

Ralph could easily spend an hour analysing each one, trying to work out why it made people laugh. It wasn't just the joke itself, it was the way people told it.

'Take Coill and Legge,' Ralph said, the day after he had watched a performance by the famous pair. 'When they sing their funny songs, Coill is always winking and making faces, but Legge is always serious, as if he can't understand what's so funny. And that *makes* it funny.'

'Maybe it's just Coill's faces that are funny,' Antonio suggested.

'Do you think so? Next time I'll block my ears so I can't hear the song.'

But it wasn't just Coill's faces.

'It wasn't funny at all,' Ralph reported a couple of days later, as they were wheeling their bikes out for a ride. 'Without the song, her faces just looked stupid. But as soon as you listened, they were as funny as anything!'

Antonio nodded. He wasn't surprised.

'You should come with me one day,' said Ralph. 'I'll get you in. I'll say you've been hired to pick up the sweet packets and ice-cream cups after the show.'

'But that's collecting rubbish!'

'So?'

'I don't want to collect rubbish. That's a terrible job.'

'Antonio,' said Ralph, in a serious tone, 'you can't expect to start from the top. Look at me. I started off selling ice-creams and now I help the man who repairs the scenery.'

'Well, I'm still not going to collect rubbish,' Antonio muttered, getting on his bike.

They didn't get very far. Almost at once, they heard Mr Carman's voice behind him.

'Antonio! Wait!'

They stopped and looked back. There was Mr

Carman, in the archway, beckoning to Antonio. He had been running and his face was red.

Ralph watched as Antonio turned and rode back to Mr Carman.

'Antonio,' said Mr Carman, breathing heavily. 'I've been trying to catch you.'

'Why?'

'Mr Guzman wants to see you.'

'Mr Guzman?' A tingle of excitement raced up Antonio's spine. Finally, after all this time, Mr Guzman had sent for him. 'When?'

'Now.'

'*Now?*' cried Antonio. 'Right now? But I'm not ready.'

'Why? Can't you ride your bike another time?'

'No, you don't understand. He said he'd give me warning. He said—'

Antonio stopped. Mr Carman was watching him with a grin.

'Right now, Antonio. Mr Guzman was very precise. He told me, as soon as I find you, I must bring you to him. Come, he is waiting.'

CHAPTER 18

Mr Guzman opened the blue door of his apartment and
Antonio went into the hallway, where the man in the
painting with the three-cornered hat watched everyone
who came and went. But Mr Guzman did not take him
back into the wood-panelled room that led to the theatre.
Instead, he opened the door of another room.

Antonio had hardly taken a step, he had barely
uttered a word.

Mr Guzman laughed. 'What, Antonio, did you think
we were going back to the theatre today? I told you I
would give you warning. Besides, look at me. Am I
dressed for your performance?'

Mr Guzman was not wearing one of his dark suits,
but flannel trousers and a grey cardigan. Antonio had
never seen him dressed like this before. He still looked
very elegant, but different. You would never call him a
Homburger if you saw him dressed like this.

'But Mr Carman said . . .'

'Mr Carman said that I wanted to see you. And that is
true. Now, come. I need your advice.'

The room into which they went was as messy as all

the other rooms in Mr Guzman's apartment were neat. It was a workroom.

As soon as he stepped into it, there was a woody smell that reminded Antonio of the sap on the trees behind Duke's House, and another smell, more pungent and heady, that was like the smell in Professor Kettering's study one year when some men had come and stuck up new wallpaper. The floor was covered with wood shavings and used sandpaper scraps. In the middle of the workroom stood a long table and around the walls there were tools hanging from nails and piled in boxes. There were shelves with pots of paints, and bottles of turpentine, and jars of brushes, and stacks of sandpaper and bundles of oilstained rags. Planks of wood were stacked in one corner. On the worktable there were more tools, chisels and planes and saws and gouges and files and instruments that looked like hooked knives and other tools that Antonio could not even name.

And amongst all the tools and scraps on the table there were four carved figures.

Two of the figures were fully painted, gleaming with

colour just like the figures in the theatre. One was plain wood. The other was only partially carved. Above the waist it was a person, with arms, head and body, and below the waist it was still a square block of wood.

Antonio recognised them immediately, even the one that had not fully emerged from its block. That one was Shoshi, wearing a beret on her head. The two painted figures were Willi Brindle and Paul Snee. Mr Guzman had exaggerated Willi Brindle's size, and maybe he had exaggerated Paul Snee's roundness.

'That is part of their characters,' said Mr Guzman, when Antonio pointed this out. 'We are not making figures of your friends, Antonio, we are making figures of the characters. It is possible that your friends did not fit the characters exactly.'

Antonio picked up Paul Snee and examined his face. Paul was scowling and puffing out his red cheeks.

'He looks . . . angrier than I remember.'

'He *was* angry,' said Mr Guzman.

'As angry as that?'

'If he played the part again, Antonio, he would be even angrier. It was an angry part.'

'I don't think it was meant to be,' said Antonio, trying to remember exactly what it was they had planned beside the duckpond. 'Maybe it was just a bit angry.'

'But that is the theatre, Antonio. It makes everything bigger, hotter than real life. You can't stay just a bit angry, or a bit sad. If you are angry, then . . .' Mr Guzman snapped his fingers, 'you are *angry*. Properly. That's why it fascinates us.'

Antonio examined Willi, and Shoshi, whose body melted into wood, and Ralph, who was not yet painted, as thin as a stick and as tall as a beanstalk, clutching a hunk of cheese in one hand and a length of celery in the other. And then he noticed that there was a fifth block on the table that was yet to be carved. Within that block, he knew, was the last figure of the play, waiting for Mr Guzman's chisel to release it. It was Antonio himself.

'We need to decide on the scenery,' said Mr Guzman. 'That was why I asked Mr Carman to bring you. I need your advice.'

'But *Four Stories* didn't have any scenery,' said Antonio.

'No. Of course, we could just paint some grass and the sky, as it really was. But for an inside theatre, Antonio, that would look quite artificial.'

Antonio thought. 'We could put the Duke's House in the scenery,' he suggested.

'True,' said Mr Guzman. 'That would make it more interesting.'

Mr Guzman took Antonio into the room with the armchairs and the watercolour pictures of wildflowers. He went out again and returned with a jug of his lime lemonade.

'The point about scenery,' said Mr Guzman, as he poured the lemonade, 'is that it must fit the play. Your idea of the play. It is not necessarily best to show exactly where the action happened. Sometimes, showing something else in the background contributes more to the idea.'

Antonio nodded, thinking. He drank two whole glasses of Mr Guzman's lemonade as he thought. Mr Guzman was right. The more you drank his lemonade, the more you liked it.

'I once did a play where we just had blank walls,' said Mr Guzman. 'It was a very stark play.'

Antonio did not think that blank walls would be right for *Four Stories*. 'What about having a different scenery for each place? The room, the concert hall, the restaurant.'

Mr Guzman considered the idea. 'Perhaps. But any designer will tell you, more scenery doesn't make a better play. The right scenery, however much of it there is, that is what you want.'

They thought some more. Mr Guzman had a second glass of lemonade as well.

Eventually Mr Guzman said: 'There are some theatres where the audience sits right around the stage, on every side. The actors come and go through the middle of them. There isn't any scenery. There are just a few sticks of furniture on the stage, a table, a chair, whatever is needed.' Mr Guzman looked enquiringly at Antonio. 'What do you think?'

Antonio considered.

'It would be the equivalent of the way the play was originally performed,' Mr Guzman said, 'but for an inside theatre.'

'Yes,' said Antonio.

Mr Guzman got a pad and a pencil and made a quick sketch. He showed it to Antonio.

'You see, instead of painting a scene on the background, we paint a crowd looking on, seated in a semicircle. In fact, we can put them in a room like the theatre itself, as if there is just such another room on the other side of the stage.'

Mr Guzman flipped the page and made another rough sketch on the pad. It didn't take more than a minute. He held it out to Antonio.

'Yes,' said Antonio, looking at the sketch. He could just imagine how it would look in Mr Guzman's theatre. It was perfect. He put down his glass. 'Shall we paint it now?' he asked enthusiastically, ready to jump up and rush back to the workroom.

Mr Guzman laughed. 'Not now, Antonio. I have been carving all morning and I am far too tired. But it does me good to hear you say such things. I was the same when I was a boy, exactly the same. I never stopped for a second. Fortunately, you are still too young to know what it is to be too old and tired.'

Antonio looked at Mr Guzman. That strange, sad feeling came over him again, as it did the first time he spoke with Mr Guzman on the stone bench outside Duke's House.

'You're not too old, Mr Guzman,' he said.

'No? Well, I am tired. Anyway, you will have to wait a little more, Antonio. Do you have enough patience?'

'Yes.'

Mr Guzman nodded. He dropped the sketch pad on the table and leaned back in his chair. He closed his eyes, breathing slowly.

Antonio looked at the sketch. He thought about the workroom, and the carved and painted figures that stood on the table there. All of Mr Guzman's preparations were so careful, they would recreate the play just as it was, or even better than it was when it had actually been performed. But what was the use of this if he, Antonio, could not remember all the parts and lines of the play? Mr Guzman's work would be wasted.

Antonio glanced up at Mr Guzman. Mr Guzman's eyes were still closed. He looked back guiltily at the sketch. He could imagine perfectly what the scenery would look like once Mr Guzman had painted it.

'Mr Guzman?'

Mr Guzman looked up.

Antonio still hesitated. 'Mr Guzman, I've been trying to remember the play.'

'And?'

'Well . . . I can't remember it all. Not every word.'

'So?' said Mr Guzman.

'So . . . I just think you should know. If I can't remember all the lines, how will I be able to perform it?'

Mr Guzman gazed at Antonio for a moment, as if giving him the chance to answer his own question.

'Think, Antonio. How will you be able to perform it?'

'I don't know. I never wrote it down. If I had written it down, there wouldn't be a problem.'

'Is that what you think? Well, Antonio, if that's the case, it's too late to do anything about it now.'

Antonio frowned. 'You said you would help me, Mr Guzman.'

'I have already helped you.'

Antonio was surprised. 'When did you help me?'

'Don't you remember?'

Antonio shook his head.

'The very first day I spoke to you, Antonio. You asked me a question. You asked whether I knew the words of every character I had played. Do you remember? What did I say?'

Antonio thought. 'You said all you had to do was think about what they were like.'

'Yes. All you have to do is to remember who is the character that you are playing. If you know what he is like, what he is *really* like, if you have that in your head, the words will come.'

'Is that all?'

'Is that all? Isn't that enough?' Mr Guzman laughed. He stood up. 'It is more than it sounds. Wait here, Antonio.'

Mr Guzman walked slowly out of the room. When he came back, he was carrying the carved figure of Paul

Snee in his hand. He put it on the table beside the sketch pad and sat down again.

'Look at him, Antonio.'

Antonio looked. Paul Snee gazed angrily back.

'Think of who he is. What he feels, what he thinks, what he sees. He sees you! He is looking at you. Now see *yourself*, Antonio, through his eyes.'

Antonio glanced sharply at Mr Guzman. Mr Guzman nodded.

'You are now a boy who is trying to tell jokes and can't remember them. You see another boy looking at you. You are frustrated. You are angry. Can you feel it?'

Antonio stared at Paul Snee's figure, trying to feel his anger.

'Forget the words, understand the character. When you come back to the theatre, you will see the figures on the stage. Do not simply look *at* them. Use them. They can help you. Put yourself inside them and look *out*. Feel the wood of the stage under your feet. The stage is now your world. The figures are your fellows. You walk amongst them.' Mr Guzman paused. He removed the figure from the table and waited until Antonio looked up at him. 'Does that help, Antonio? Think about it some more. Think about the characters, imagine how it will feel to see with their eyes. That's the important part. Don't worry about the words. It isn't important to have them written down. They will come out by themselves.'

Antonio nodded, but he was not very certain. Mr Guzman made it sound so easy. But what if the words didn't come out by themselves?

Mr Guzman smiled. 'Good. Come back next Thursday, at three.'

Antonio couldn't come on Thursday at three. School was starting again.

'Then come the following Saturday, at two-thirty.'

'All right.'

'All right.' said Mr Guzman. 'When you come back on Saturday, everything will be ready. You must be ready as well.'

Ralph Robinson couldn't go to the Variety Theatre during the week now that school had started again. He could only go to the Saturday afternoon performances.

'I'll get you in with me tomorrow,' he said to Antonio, as they were walking home from school on Friday afternoon. 'I'll say you've been hired to help little old ladies get to their seats.'

'No.'

'Why not? I'm not asking you to collect rubbish. Besides, you don't actually have to do it. The little old ladies can look after themselves once we get inside.'

'No.'

'Why not? It took me ages to think up that scheme.'

'Because I can't.'

'Why can't you?'

'Because I'm busy.'

'What are you busy with?'

'I'm just busy.'

'Well, I may just be too busy to ever think up another idea for you,' said Ralph, punching him on the arm.

On Saturday afternoon Ralph Robinson went to watch the show at the Variety Theatre. And Antonio S went to the theatre of Theodore Guzman.

'Are you ready?' said Mr Guzman.

Antonio nodded.

Mr Guzman settled down on one of the benches. He was dressed in his most elegant suit, wearing his finest silk tie, and his polished shoes reflected the light of the lantern hanging from the roof.

'Take your time, Antonio. I will help you.'

In front of Antonio, the stage was lit. Another, painted audience looked out at him. There were two figures on the stage. A girl with a black beret and her arms crossed over her chest, standing at one of the front corners of the stage, and a long thin boy with a hunk of cheese in one hand and a stick of celery in the other.

Antonio tried to remember everything that Mr Guzman had told him. He tried to understand the characters.

He took a deep breath.

'Marcia Riley,' he said, giving the name they had used for Shoshi Vargaz in *Four Stories*. He could hear his voice wavering. 'She cannot speak. She writes songs.'

'Yes, Antonio. She writes songs of the things she cannot say,' suggested Mr Guzman.

'Yes,' said Antonio. 'But the songs have never been sung. She has never heard her songs.'

'Except in her own mind,' said Mr Guzman. 'Think as the characters, Antonio. In her mind, Marcia hears the songs. In her mind, she hears them in the sweetest, most beautiful voice the world has ever heard.'

Antonio nodded. Mr Guzman was right. In her own mind, Marcia must hear the songs as if someone were singing them perfectly.

'Saul Riley,' he said, using the name for Ralph Robinson's character. 'Marcia's brother. Always hungry. Knows how to talk a lot. Knows how to get food from anybody by talking.'

'Talks enough to make up for Marcia's silence,' suggested Mr Guzman.

'Maybe,' said Antonio. 'He knows how to eat enough to make up for Marcia's appetite, that's for sure. She eats like a sparrow. Half her food always ends up being given to the dog.'

'And Saul eats like a horse.'

'Yes. A sparrow and a horse. That's what they are.'

Mr Guzman laughed. 'Exactly, Antonio. A sparrow and a thin, hungry horse.'

Antonio paused. He glanced at Mr Guzman for an instant, took another deep breath, and began.

'I'm hungry. I'm terribly, teeeeerribly hungry. It must be three hours to go until dinnertime. And I'm hungry! I know what you're thinking, Marcia. "He's always hungry—"'

'Antonio,' said Mr Guzman, 'wait. What is Saul doing as he speaks? Is he moving? Is he still? Where is he looking?'

'He is looking at Marcia.'

'Then you must tell me. *You* are each character. You must think, speak, act for each one. Now, tell me.'

Saul Riley is looking at Marcia. He says: 'I know what you're—'

'No, Antonio. You must try harder. How is Saul speaking? Softly? Loudly? Dejectedly? Hopefully?'

'Dejectedly.'

'Very good. Then you must speak dejectedly. You are his voice. He has no other. Now, what does he say in this dejected tone?'

'I know what—'

'Harder, Antonio. Think of the character. Use the figure on the stage. Let him help you. You are inside him. Remember? You are looking *out*.'

Antonio concentrated. He gazed at the figure of Saul Riley in front of him.

'Inside him, Antonio. Who do you see? Marcia Riley. And you are . . .'

'Hungry. Very hungry.'

Something was happening. Suddenly, Antonio felt

that he was beginning to understand what Mr Guzman really meant. The thin figure on the stage was gnawed with hunger. Antonio could feel the hunger within him. He could feel the wood of the stage under his feet. He was starting to see with Saul Riley's eyes. Marcia was in front of him.

'Antonio, what does he say in his dejected tone?'

The seconds passed. This new feeling was almost frightening.

'Antonio? Tell me!'

'I know what you're thinking, Marcia: "He's always hungry."'

'Yes. What else?'

'"He eats enough for three growing boys, and he's always hungry." That's what you're thinking, isn't it? Well, it's true, Marcia, I'm always hungry. Do you think it's easy always being hungry? You're never hungry, are you?'

'What does Marcia do?'

She shakes her head. 'You're lucky, Marcia,' Saul says.

'Is Saul still standing there?' Mr Guzman asked.

Saul sits down next to Marcia. 'You're lucky, Marcia,' he says.

Marcia shakes her head again.

'Well, of course you can't talk. So you're not that lucky.'

'And what does—'

'Saul laughs!' said Antonio before Mr Guzman could

even finish his question, without even looking around. It was obvious. Mr Guzman smiled to himself. He looked back at the stage.

Saul laughs. It's not because Marcia can't talk, but it's . . . the way he said that she was lucky.

'*I can't get enough to put in my mouth, and you can't get anything to come out of your mouth. What a pair! Like a sparrow and a horse. We should be partners.*'

Saul is very unhappy. Suddenly Marcia pulls her pad out of her pocket. You see, Marcia never goes anywhere without her pad and pen, it's the only way she can talk with people. That's how she communicates. She writes something now.

Saul laughs. 'What do you mean, "Let's be partners"?'

Marcia grabs the pad back and writes some more.

Saul reads. 'You be my mouth, and I'll give you my food.' He looks up at Marcia. 'All your food? I couldn't take all your food, Marcia. I couldn't take more than, about, three quarters.'

Marcia nods.

Suddenly Saul gets suspicious. 'What do you mean: "You be my mouth"?'

Marcia writes again.

'"*Sing my songs*"? *Sing your songs, Marcia? No, that's not fair. I hate singing. Look, instead of three quarters of your food, just give me half. All right? I'll settle for that. Just don't make me sing.*'

Marcia grabs her pad back.

Saul gets up. He's very angry. He's even more hungry than before. He's really mad. You see, Marcia has a biscuit in her pocket and Saul knows she's got it. But he hates singing. People laugh at him when he sings.

Saul comes back to Marcia. He says: 'I think I'd better taste your food before I make this decision.'

Marcia rolls her eyes. Saul doesn't have to taste anything. Saul knows exactly what she's got, because he gets exactly the same food himself. So Marcia takes the biscuit out of her pocket and only breaks off a tiny piece. And Saul ... Saul . . . He kneels in front of her hand. Right on his knees! He takes the little piece and he pops it in his mouth and rolls on the floor, rubbing his stomach. Just like a dog. That's how much he likes to eat! Then he says: 'All right, I'll do it. I'll sing your songs. Just give me the rest of the biscuit.'

Now Marcia writes something.

Saul reads it. '"Let me hear a song first." No, I'm too hungry to sing now, Mabbs. Give me the rest of the biscuit and I'll sing then.'

Marcia gives him the rest of the biscuit and Saul gobbles it up. Now she's waiting.

'I'm too full to sing now, Mabbs. Later on.'

Marcia is angry. Very, very angry. She turns and faces the wall. Saul watches her. It won't be long before he's hungry again. One biscuit doesn't go far in Saul Riley's stomach!

He says: 'Marcia, I can't sing, you know that. You've heard me try.'

Marcia just . . . she just shrugs.

'What if I find someone who will sing for you, Mabbs?'

Marcia turns around. She doesn't believe him.

'Will you still give me three quarters of your food?'

Marcia doesn't write anything. She just watches him. Because she doesn't completely trust him.

'Do you know—'

Saul stops himself just in time. He has a great idea. He walks to the other side of the stage, where Marcia can't hear him.

'Bozie Tucker would give anything to sing Mabbs's songs. Bozie Tucker thinks she has the loveliest voice around. She's got the loudest voice, that's for sure. If I give one of Mabbs's songs to Bozie Tucker, I'll probably get one of her mother's cream cakes. Maybe two. Bozie's mother makes the best cream cakes I've ever tasted.'

And then Saul frowns.

'But if I tell Mabbs about Bozie Tucker, and Mabbs goes there herself, I won't get anything from Bozie. I may not even get anything from Mabbs. What I need is someone to keep Mabbs occupied while I go and see Bozie.'

A big smile comes over Saul's face. Marcia is still watching him. Now his voice is very sweet. 'Just you wait here, Mabbs. I'll be back.'

And then he rushes off the stage.

Antonio turned to Mr Guzman to see what he was going to say. Mr Guzman was still watching the stage. Even after a whole minute had passed, Mr Guzman had not looked at him. Antonio realised that Mr Guzman was still deep within the play. He was not going to say anything. He had stopped helping. Antonio was alone.

He removed Marcia and put the figure of Paul Snee next to Saul Riley. He stopped to concentrate for a moment, looking at the figures, trying to feel as they felt, to look outwards through their eyes, to feel the wood of the stage under his feet. And then, a minute later, he had started speaking and was deep within their world.

For the rest of the afternoon, Antonio was not aware of anything else. He was not aware of himself, of Mr Guzman, of the stage, the theatre, the Duke's house, of anything. He was within the characters. His voice belonged to them and his thoughts were theirs. He ceased to exist and five characters leapt into life in his place, taking their energy from him.

At the end of it, he had never been so exhausted, so drained. He was numb. The figures from the final scene, Saul Riley and the restaurant chef, stood on the stage. Antonio sat on one of the benches and stared at the floor. He felt, in a way that was not completely clear even to himself, that he had achieved something more difficult and more important than anything else he had ever done. But he did not yet have the energy to understand it.

Then he looked around.

Mr Guzman, who had never once taken his eyes off the stage through the whole play, was on his feet. He was clapping his slow, resounding claps. Not just three times, as he had clapped on the lawn outside the Duke's house, but on and on and on.

CHAPTER 20

Mr Guzman had stopped clapping. He was sitting next to Antonio.

'I was right,' he said.

Antonio didn't know what he meant.

'To show you the theatre. I was certainly right. But I never really doubted it, Antonio.'

'Yes, Mr Guzman.'

Mr Guzman chuckled. 'It is not so easy, to perform a whole play like that. You have found that out. But there is no other satisfaction like it in the world. By tomorrow, when you are full of energy again, you will agree.' Mr Guzman gazed at Antonio for a moment longer. The smile lingered on his face. 'And now, with your permission, we must put your play in the theatre.'

Mr Guzman went to one of the cabinets and opened the door. There were not as many boards in this cabinet as there had been in the others that Antonio had seen, and there were empty niches on the inside of the door.

'Here there is room for one more play.'

Mr Guzman went back to the stage and removed the

background for *Four Stories*. He placed it in the cabinet, leaning against the other boards.

'Bring the figures, Antonio.'

Antonio brought over the figure of Marcia Riley, but Mr Guzman did not take it.

'The first one, Antonio. The first one to speak goes in first.'

Antonio brought the stick-like figure of Saul Riley and Mr Guzman put it in the first free spot. Then Antonio brought the other figures and Mr Guzman laid them carefully on the green felt of their niches.

'Now the board, Antonio. The boards go in order of the scenes. Do you understand?'

Antonio nodded.

'Good. You must remember this, otherwise you won't know how to use the theatre.' Mr Guzman closed the cabinet door. 'Now we must enter your play in the key. You see, *I* know what is in the theatre, but without the key, no one else does. If you do not where the key is, the theatre is of no use to you.'

Mr Guzman went back to the stage. He went down creakily on his knees and pressed the middle of the rose that was carved there. The panel swung out noiselessly on a hinge. Inside was another panel covered in a sheet of cream-coloured paper.

'This is the key,' said Mr Guzman.

Antonio knelt beside Mr Guzman. The contents of

every cabinet in the theatre were listed on the paper. Each cabinet had a number and against this number were listed the titles of the plays that it contained, and against each title were listed the names of the producer, the director, the set designer, the costume designer, the lighting designer, the number of boards and the number of figures. The year of each production was listed as well. Some of the productions were forty years old.

The writing on the paper was very beautiful, with perfectly formed letters and not a single blot.

'The plays in each cabinet are listed backwards,' said Mr Guzman, lifting out the panel with the paper. 'The plays that are at the top of the list are deepest in the cabinet. Do you understand?'

'Yes,' said Antonio.

Mr Guzman took out the panel. He carried it to one of the benches and sat down. He took a gold fountain pen from inside his jacket. Resting the board on his knees, he began to write.

Underneath the three plays already listed against cabinet number six, Mr Guzman wrote *Four Stories*. Antonio watched the pen and could hear the nib scratching the surface of the paper as it formed the words. It was the same careful, elegant handwriting in which the details of the other plays were written.

In the spaces for producer and director, Mr Guzman wrote 'Antonio S'. In the spaces for the designers, he wrote 'Theodore Guzman'. He wrote the year. It was twenty-one years later than the previous play on the list.

Mr Guzman put his pen away. He blew on the paper to make sure that the ink was dry.

'Would you please return this to its place,' he said to Antonio, handing him the panel.

Antonio took the panel and slotted it back into position under the stage.

'And now gently close the door.'

Hesitantly, Antonio swung the outer panel back. He felt it catch.

'And now show me how you open it, Antonio. But gently. Everything must be done gently. It is a delicate mechanism. I made it myself.'

The centre of the rose moved in under his fingers, and the panel swung out.

'Good,' said Mr Guzman, 'so now you know.'

Antonio closed the panel once more. He stood up.

'Now tell me, do you remember, Antonio, in the key the plays are listed ...'

'Backwards. And the first figure to speak is placed first, and the boards are in order of the scenes.'

'Yes,' said Mr Guzman. 'If you can remember this,

and if you can remember how to get to the key, you will know how to use the theatre. Nothing can stop you. Then, Antonio, the only limit will be the limit of your own imagination.'

'I remember already,' said Antonio.

'Tell me again.'

Antonio told him the arrangement of the theatre.

'And be gentle with the mechanism. Always be gentle with it.'

'Yes, Mr Guzman.'

Mr Guzman nodded. He closed his eyes. He looked tired and worn, but there was an expression of great peacefulness on his face.

'When will you tell me some more of the plays?' asked Antonio.

'Soon,' he said.

'When?' asked Antonio.

'You are impatient, Antonio,' said Mr Guzman, opening his eyes. 'Why? There is no need to rush. You have the key. You do not really need me now.'

Antonio could not imagine ever being able to tell a play like Mr Guzman.

'When will you tell me some more of the plays?' he asked again.

Mr Guzman smiled. 'Well, not today, Antonio, I am far too tired. Come back next week, on Sunday, at two.'

CHAPTER 21

Mr Guzman was not at home on Sunday at two. Antonio knocked on his door and waited for him, knowing how slow he was to answer. But Mr Guzman didn't appear and eventually Antonio knocked again. Finally he left. He came back the next day after school, and this time Mr Carman saw him. There was no use knocking on Mr Guzman's door, he told him. Mr Guzman had been in the hospital since Friday.

Antonio waited for Professor Kettering to come home. She came home late and Scarrabo cooked her an omelette. Antonio asked if Mr Guzman was in the hospital.

'Yes,' said Professor Kettering.

'How long has he been there?'

'For about three days, Antonio.'

Scarrabo tipped the omelette onto a plate and put it in front of Professor Kettering.

'Are you looking after him?' asked Antonio.

'Yes,' said Professor Kettering, turning the handle of the pepper grinder.

'Mama, is he very sick?'

Professor Kettering looked up. She glanced at Scarrabo before answering.

'Yes, Antonio, he is very sick.'

The next day, Antonio was in Professor Kettering's study when she came home. He fiddled with the bones of her skeleton as he waited. As soon as she came in he asked her whether Mr Guzman was getting better.

'I'm afraid not,' said Professor Kettering.

She sat down at her desk and looked at Antonio sadly. She reached out a hand and Antonio came to her and Professor Kettering put an arm around him.

'Mr Guzman is very sick, Antonio. He has been sick for a long time, but he didn't see anyone. He didn't want to see a doctor.'

'He saw me,' said Antonio.

'Then you are lucky, Antonio. That will be something to remember.'

'Mama, will you be able to cure Mr Guzman?'

Professor Kettering shook her head. 'I don't think so, Antonio. He is very sick.'

Antonio frowned. 'Do you see him at the hospital, Mama?'

'Yes, I see him each day.'

'Will you tell him something for me?'

'What, Antonio?'

'Tell him I remember.'

Professor Kettering gave Antonio a puzzled look. 'What do you remember?'

'Just tell him I remember. Mr Guzman will understand. Tell him I remember the key.'

'What key?'

'Will you tell him, Mama?'

'I don't understand, Antonio.'

'Will you tell him? Yes? Promise?'

'All right, Antonio. I'll tell him.'

'What will you tell him? Tell me exactly.'

'I will tell him that Antonio S remembers the key.'

'Promise?'

'Promise.'

'Thank you, Mama.'

A few days later Professor Kettering came home and sat down with Antonio and told him that Mr Guzman had died in the hospital. He had been very sick, and there was nothing that could be done to save him.

Antonio had never really known anyone who had died. Scarrabo's mother had died when he was a baby, but he couldn't remember her at all. Sometimes he thought about Mr Guzman, and his neat, methodical apartment with the messy workroom in which he had carved so skilfully. He thought about the strangely wonderful theatre in which the only limit was the limit of your own imagination. But most of all he remembered the sound of Mr Guzman's voice, so deep and expressive, that could make the characters in any story, any play, come alive.

Antonio did not think of Mr Guzman all the time. It was only sometimes, perhaps late at night before he went to sleep, or if he happened to be walking home by himself from school. Most of the time there were plenty of other things to keep him occupied. For instance, Ralph Robinson's brother Randolph had just got a bike and Antonio and Ralph were teaching him to ride. Within a week they had him off his training wheels, although he was still falling off when he went round the corner under the archway too quickly. And there was the invention room, where Scarrabo and Walter Flood and Louisa Roberts were hard at work again, planning the performances for Scarrabo's autumn shows. They had to invent at least five new tricks every season, and each year it was harder to think of new ideas than the year before. And Antonio even started going to the Variety Theatre with Ralph Robinson on Saturday afternoons. Ralph told the man on the door that Antonio was there to sell programs.

The man on the door believed anything Ralph told him.

One morning there was a van parked in the courtyard near Mr Guzman's old apartment. Antonio saw it when he was leaving for school. The weather was already starting to get cold again and the morning air was crisp. Antonio put his hands deep in his pockets, waiting for Ralph Robinson. Two men came out of the apartment carrying an armchair. Antonio recognised the gold tassels on the cushions. It was one of the armchairs from the room with the fireplace, where he had drunk Mr Guzman's lime lemonade.

Ralph came down the stairs and stopped beside Antonio. For a few minutes they stood and watched the removals men coming in and out with furniture.

'Did you hear? The Homburger's dead,' said Ralph. 'I heard my mother say so a couple of days ago.'

'I know,' Antonio replied.

'He was so old he probably just fell over and died one day.'

Antonio didn't reply.

'They've sold his apartment. Looks like they're moving his stuff out.'

The men came out again. This time they had the white sofa. Antonio turned away and left for school.

When he came back in the afternoon the truck was gone. Mr Carman was polishing the gold handle on the door of the apartment. The new owners would soon be moving in. Mr Carman didn't know where the removals men had taken Mr Guzman's furniture. Maybe it was all going to be sold in a big auction.

Antonio climbed the stairs. What would the new owners do with the alchemy room? They would never know what its real use was. They would probably put in a window or knock another door into one of the walls and ruin the proportions. And what would happen to the theatre at the auction? People would probably think that the figures were dolls, and that the cabinets were just plain old cupboards, and maybe someone would buy the stage for puppet shows. And even if one person bought all the parts of the theatre, he would never know how to use it. Now that Mr Guzman was dead, Antonio was the only person in the whole world who knew the key.

Scarrabo was on the stairs to the tower when Antonio came in.

'Antonio, something came for you today,' he said.

'What?'

'Come with me,' said Scarrabo, turning upstairs.

Antonio followed Scarrabo through Professor Kettering's study and up to the invention room.

'Here he is,' said Walter Flood. 'We've spent the whole afternoon bringing your stuff upstairs!'

'What stuff?' asked Antonio, looking around. He couldn't see anything new in the invention room.

'We put it in the loft,' said Scarrabo. 'You should have seen the trouble we had getting it up there, but there wasn't room anywhere else.'

'There was hardly room for it in the loft,' added Walter Flood.

Antonio followed Scarrabo up the narrow staircase to the loft. Scarrabo stopped with his hand on the door handle.

'Don't you know who it's from, Antonio?' he asked.

'No.'

'Are you sure? Think carefully.'

Scarrabo opened the door.

The loft was dark. Antonio peered into the shadows.

Scarrabo switched on the light.

It was the theatre of Theodore Guzman. The walnut-wood stage stood in the middle of the loft, and on each side of it, in two rows of three, were the six cabinets. The two leather benches were between them, one resting upside down on top of the other. All around were Scarrabo's boxes and chests, and the pieces of the theatre were crowded close to one another, but they were all there.

'What is it, Antonio?' asked Walter Flood, who had come up the stairs behind him with Louisa Roberts.

'A theatre,' said Antonio.

'A theatre?'

'It's quite small,' said Louisa Roberts.

'Yes,' said Antonio. 'Papa, will you take this bench down?'

Scarrabo and Walter lifted the top bench down and rested it on the ground. Now there was barely an inch of empty space in the loft.

'Thank you,' said Antonio.

Then he turned around and went back through the invention room and the study and down to the kitchen, where he poured himself a glass of orange juice.

Walter Flood followed him all the way down.

'Antonio, don't you want to look at it?' he asked.

'I know what it is,' said Antonio.

'I wish I did,' said Walter, as he turned to go back to the invention room.

Antonio drank his orange juice. Then he did some geography homework. Then he went out and wandered around in the wood behind Duke's House with Mr Carman's brown labrador dog, who would retrieve any stick you threw unless she happened to come across the scent of a squirrel on her way back.

Of course, Antonio did want to look at the theatre in the loft. But he wanted to look at it alone.

After dinner Antonio climbed up to the loft and turned on the light and closed the door behind him.

He sat on one of the leather benches and looked at the stage for a while. Its triangular top almost scraped the rafters. He let his eyes wander over the thick, rich carving. Then he got up and opened the door of one of the cabinets, and without even stopping to see what it showed he pulled out the first board and climbed over a box to get to the side of the stage.

There was just enough room to open the side panel and slot the board in. Then he went back to the cabinet and grabbed the two closest figures from the door and put them on the stage in front of it.

Antonio didn't check the key. Right now, that wasn't important.

He sat down again. At the back of the stage, there was the wall of a castle, with a gateway that was closed by a heavy portcullis. It must have been night, because there were lighted torches burning brightly along the battlements. In front stood a jester who was dressed in a suit of red and blue diamonds and a silly floppy hat with a bell on the end. The other figure was an old fisherman in rags with a red nose and a fishing line slung over his shoulder.

Antonio didn't know what play the board and the figures came from.

He stared for a long time at the two figures in front of the castle wall, just as he had stared at the figures on the stage when he performed in the theatre of Theodore Guzman. The carving was so detailed, the colours were so expressive. Already, he could tell so much about the characters. Already he was beginning to know them, to be able to see through their eyes.

'A jester,' he murmured. 'Always making jokes for other people.'

He thought some more.

'A fisherman. Always catching fish for other people. The sea is always cold. So cold that his nose is always red.'

Antonio gazed at the scenery.

'It is night. They are outside. They have arrived too late. They have been locked out of the castle.'

Antonio laughed.

What a story! A jester and a fisherman locked out of a castle for the night. Well, maybe they had been. Or maybe they would be.

It didn't feel the same as Mr Guzman's theatre. It was just a cluttered loft. It wasn't that special, stark room with the eight walls and the tall pointed ceiling and the lantern hanging down. But Antonio remembered, he had the key. And Mr Guzman himself had said, a theatre is wherever you happen to perform.